Tim Wright is the co-host, along with Dr Michael Gurian, of *The Wonder of Parenting Podcast: A Brain-Science Approach to Parenting.* He and his wife, Jan, live in Glendale, Arizona. They have two adult children and five grandchildren. Tim is an avid fan of the Arizona Cardinals.

Praise for The Adventures of Toby Baxter Book 2: *RiverHome for the Holidays*

Serious, jolly, and instructive—an entertaining Christmas adventure in the best spirit of the season.

–Kirkus Reviews

A fun, imaginative, and vibrant story full of high action and wordplay... A must-read middle grade fantasy.

—The Prairies Book Review

RiverHome for the Holidays delivers a captivating blend of humor, danger, and inspiration. For lovers of fantasy with mythical creatures, this book is a must-read, promising a thrilling and heartwarming adventure. Dive into the enchanting world of *RiverHome* alongside Toby Baxter – you won't be disappointed! Reading With Your Kids Certified Great Read.

–readingwithyourkids.com

Tim Wright's new book, *The Adventures of Toby Baxter—Book 2: RiverHome for the Holidays*, once again invites middle-school age readers and their families into an engaging, humorous, and insightful fantasy adventure.

—Dr. Michael Gurian, New York Times Best- Selling Author of The Wonder of Boys *and* The Stone Boys.

Jennifer –

Tim Wright

THE ADVENTURES OF
TOBY BAXTER

BOOK 2

RIVERHOME
FOR THE HOLIDAYS

Think Scrooge!

[signature]

THE ADVENTURES OF TOBY BAXTER

Books in the series:
Book 1: The River Elf, the Giant, and the Closet

Book 2: RiverHome for the Holidays

Free Prequels
Book 1 Prequel: *I.C.E. Call Toby Baxter*
Book 2 Prequel: *'Twas the Night Before RiverHome*
(Free prequels available at www.TimWrightbooks.com)

THE ADVENTURES OF
TOBY BAXTER

BOOK 2

RIVERHOME FOR THE HOLIDAYS

To Toby's Fans:
Be Curious
Be Smart
Be Kind
Be Resilient

Sign up at www.TimWrightBooks.com to receive the free Book 1 Prequel: *I.C.E. Call Toby Baxter;* the Book 2 Prequel: *'Twas the Night Before RiverHome;* and stay up-to-date on the Adventures of Toby Baxter!

Contents

A Christmas Carol
By Charles Dickens

Toby opened the book and began to read:
Marley was dead, to begin with.
Skimming… skipping…
Old Marley was as dead as a door-nail.

Toby Baxter closed the book, placed it on the night stand next to his bed, and sighed. He'd been so proud of himself a few months ago when he'd actually finished reading *The Hobbit* for English Literature class. It was no easy task as he wasn't much of a book reader. He preferred *Marvel* comic books. He had hundreds of them sitting on the shelves above his desk, many of them as yet unread from his birthday haul a few months ago.

A Christmas Carol by Charles Dickens, the story of Ebenezer Scrooge, was his mom's favorite Christmas book. She'd asked if he might read it along with her in December. He wished he had said no. The old-style English of the book made it tough sledding. And those unread comic books were calling his name!

He turned off the light on his night stand and closed his eyes.

As Toby Baxter fell asleep, the sword *Loach*, hanging on his wall, began to glow.

Prologue

You Better Watch Out

Toby Baxter stared at the clock on the wall. Thirty minutes until Winter Break... Twenty-nine minutes and fifty seconds until Winter Break... Twenty-nine minutes and forty-five seconds until Winter Break... Each second felt like an eternity.

Mrs Grayson, his English Literature teacher (and his mom's best friend—inconvenient!), was doing her best to remind the class that they would be writing a short story once Winter Break was over. She hoped that everyone would use a small bit of vacation time to think about their topic and...

Toby turned and looked out the window at the thickening clouds. So far, little snow had fallen in Minneapolis. But fingers crossed, the coming storm would dump several feet of it over the next few days.

Months earlier, Toby had stared out this same window when he saw Deckor for the first time. From the second story window, he couldn't quite tell if Deckor was a boy or a small man. He looked strangely like a hobbit from the J.R.R. Tolkien book. But it turned out that Deckor was a river elf, from a place called *RiverHome,* accessed through Toby's closet! Deckor, along with his sister, Clovor, their brother, Phoenix, and their cousins, Judah and Mathilda, had recruited Toby to help them take on Clygon and his legion of trolls.

Something in the front of the classroom caught his attention. He looked away from the window back to Mrs Grayson only to discover that Author was leading the class. He sat on the edge of the teacher's desk, a notebook in his large right hand and a pencil in his left. Through his reading glasses, he winked at Toby and scribbled something in the notebook.

Toby looked around at the other students. They all seemed frozen in time. Apparently, only Toby could see Author.

Hello, Toby! It's so good to see you again.

12

The words appeared above Author's head as he spoke them. He could see Toby looking slightly above his head and made another note in the notebook.

Author was a big man with a deep voice and dark skin. Toby believed him to be quite old, *perhaps in his fifties?* His oval head was bald. Toby couldn't tell if Author had lost his hair or liked to shave his head. But today, his head was covered by a Santa hat. His graying goatee had morphed into what looked like a Santa beard. He was wearing boots, jeans, and the ugliest ugly Christmas sweater Toby had ever seen. It was hideous. Christmas green with a snowman, Rudolph, a Christmas Tree, Christmas presents, and various kinds of shiny thingies all over it. Although, Toby had to admit, the Christmas green matched Author's eyes. *Contact lenses maybe?*

"Hey, Author. What are you doing here?"

It looks like the words are above my head once again. You know what that means.

"I'm not into the story yet. Which means… there's a story coming?"

That depends.

"On what?"

The Prologue.

"What's a Prologue?"

A Prologue introduces a story. It sets the stage for what's about to happen. It introduces the reader to the adventure up ahead, by teasing out a few of the themes that will shape the story.

"Um… okay…"

Like… Author thought for a moment. **Easter Eggs.**

"Easter Eggs?"

Apparently, hiding Easter Eggs in movies, books, and songs has become hip and groovy.

"Hip? Groovy? When were you born?"

So, putting the phrase, 'Easter Eggs' into the Prologue gets the story off and running.

"I'm not sure that's what Easter Eggs means in a…"

Easter Eggs. Check.

Author wrote something in his notebook and smiled. Then he thought some more.

Clygon.

Toby felt a surge of fear at the sound of that name.

"Clygon? What about Clygon?"

Author frowned. He wrote again in the notebook.

The Christmas Giant.

Then…

"Trouble."

The words above Author's head had disappeared.

Toby almost jumped out of his desk chair.

"Is the Christmas Giant in trouble? Does it have something to do with Clygon?"

Author closed his notebook, took off his reading glasses, and put the pencil behind his ear. "I see you are no longer looking above my head, Toby. You are now back in the story…"

"Toby! Toby Baxter! Earth to Toby!"

Toby turned his head to see Mrs Graysonlooking at him. He could feel the whole class staring at him.

"Toby, I know you're excited to start Winter Break, but before the bell rings, can you summarize for the class what a Prologue is?"

Toby could feel his face turning red. His friend, Sid, flashed him a big, goofy Sid smile. Derrick, the class bully, snickered behind him. *Why do I suddenly want a candy bar?* Toby wondered.

"A Prologue is an, um, ah, is… a way… to get… a story started. It sets the stage for what's about to happen."

"Excellent, Toby. I was sure you were daydreaming but you proved me wrong once again.

"Okay, class, I'm only giving you one small project to do during Winter Break."

The whole class, including Toby, groaned.

"Write up a Prologue for your short story. Remember, your story is due at the end of January. The Prologue doesn't have to be long. But take the time to set up…"

The bell rang.

"Have a nice vacation," Mrs Grayson shouted. But no one heard her. The class had vanished out the door into the hallway and out into the coming snow storm.

Because there had been little snow so far and the temps were mild, Toby had ridden his bike to school. Now, flying down one street after another, slowing at each intersection to check for cars, past the large round water tower at the park, up a small hill and down another to his house, Author's words chased after him: *Clygon. The Christmas Giant. Trouble.*

He quickly parked his bike in the garage and rushed into the house, past his father, who was unsuccessfully trying to bake Christmas cookies, and into his bedroom. He threw his backpack onto his bed and ran into the closet… straight into the back wall.

Hard.

Knocking him onto his back.

That was going to leave a mark.

1

Up on the House Top

Toby sat on top of the snow-covered roof of his house. His boots were firmly planted in front of him to keep him from sliding down. Rolled up under his right arm was a plastic Captain America sled. His Spider-Man wool cap sat gingerly on his head, just above the big knot on his forehead he bore from running into the back wall of his closet.

The long-coming storm had worked its magic, just in time for Winter Break. For three solid days, it had dumped snow on the Twin Cities. Lots of it. The best kind of snow. Wet enough to be sticky for snowball fights yet perfect for sledding. And the temp was just right as well. Mid-twenties and no wind.

Toby's mom was hibernating in St. Paul with her parents for a few days, leaving Toby and his dad on their own. Dad had suggested that they invite Sid for an overnight. Sid now stood at the bottom of the house, encouraging Toby to suck it up and sled down the roof.

Toby's house was built on a hill. The front of the house sat on the top of the hill, making it look like a one-story home. The backyard opened up at the bottom of the hill with a basement door leading outside.

The bottom of the front-of-the-house roof was normally eight or nine feet off the ground. But because of the snow, it was now about a four-foot drop. And hopefully nice and cushy.

The plan was for Toby to—*lie on the sled? ... lay on the sled? Why can't he ever figure that one out?*—and slide down the roof onto the ground below. No worries.

Except for that low-hanging tree branch threatening to tear off his head. And the four-foot drop into the snow.

"Come on, Toby! You've been sitting up there for ten minutes. Be a man! Get on that sled. Let's get this party rolling."

Be a man? Toby thought. I was held prisoner by trolls! I wielded a Sword! I did my bowel business in the woods! Be a man? I'll show you what a man looks like, my friend, Sid!

Toby, making sure his booted feet were firmly dug into the snow, slowly unrolled the Captain America sled behind him. He carefully leaned back onto it and lifted his head to look down his body, down the roof, down under the low-hanging-threatening-to-lop-off-his-head branch, to Sid. This suddenly didn't seem like a wise idea.

He put his head back and started to lift his feet.

"Wait! Stop!"

Uh oh. It was Toby's dad.

Toby braced himself for a "what are you thinking?" lecture from his father.

"Hang on a minute, Toby. Let me get my phone so I can record this."

"Wait... What?" Toby said. "Aren't you going to stop me?"

But nobody heard him.

"Great idea, Mr B!" said Sid.

A moment later, Dad ran back out with his phone.

"Okay, Toby! Whenever you're ready."

Toby slowly raised his left foot and then his right...

A blood-curdling scream:

HO! HO! HO! TOBY BAXTER! I'M BAAAAAACK! AND I HAVE A FRIEND OF YOURS. MERRY CHRISTMAS.

Clygon!

Toby tried to stop himself by planting his right foot into the roof. But that only caused him to spin around. Now, he couldn't get traction with either foot and found himself soaring down the roof, on his back, head first. He squeezed his eyes shut and held his breath. He flew through the air for what seemed like several minutes, thankfully landing in a cotton ball of snow.

"That was awesome!" screamed Sid. "Did you catch that on your phone, Mr B? Toby, give me the sled so I can have a try! Wow. That was amazing!"

Sid pulled the sled out from under a snow-covered Toby and started climbing the tree that would get him onto the roof for his turn.

Dad ran to Toby and pulled him up to his feet.

Toby was about to ask if his dad had heard it too. But the panic in Dad's eyes told him that, yes, Thomas Baxter had also heard Clygon's taunt.

"Hey, guys! Clear out! Sid-sational is about to fly through the air!"

They moved out of the way. Even though Toby's dad was shaking from Clygon's piercing scream, he managed to video Sid's journey down the roof.

Jumping up out of the snow, Sid shoved the sled into Toby's hands. "Woo hoo!" Sid shouted. "Let's do it again!"

Toby looked at his dad, who shrugged, put his hand on Toby's shoulder, and said, "It's all right, Toby. Go have some fun with your friend. There's nothing we can do right now."

Toby and Sid took turns sliding down the roof for the next hour. Even Dad tried it. Once.

Finally, worn out and hungry, they headed into the house for some of Dad's world-famous homemade chili, at least famous in the Baxter household. Since Sid was spending the night, Toby insisted that Sid sprinkle some Beano on each bowl of chili he ate—four bowls, Toby counted—to prevent certain disgusting sounds and noxious odors later on.

That evening, having ordered two extra-large pizzas and two huge bottles of root beer, the three of them settled in for the Monday Night Football Game. And it was a biggie. The Arizona Cardinals (Toby's favorite team) vs the Minnesota Vikings (Sid's favorite team). The game had playoff implications.

At half-time, Dad brought out some of the Christmas cookies he had tried baking a few days earlier. Though Toby and Sid had no idea what shapes the cookies were supposed to be, they didn't taste terrible.

At bedtime Sid sacked out on the floor next to Toby's bed, using Toby's Black Panther sleeping bag.

Before turning off the light, Thomas checked out his son's closet, touching the back wall to make sure that all was as it should be. Toby and his dad had said no more about Clygon, largely because, with Sid around, they didn't have the opportunity.

"Good night, men," Toby's dad said.

"Good night, Dad. Thanks for today."

"Yah... Good night, Mr B. I had lots of fun."

Toby's dad leaned down and fist-bumped Sid. Sid's dad was serving overseas and would be gone for Christmas. He was glad Sid had found a second home at the Baxter's house.

The light had been off for several minutes when Sid said, "Hey, Toby, I never knew that sword you got for your birthday glowed in the dark."

"Hmmm," Toby answered sleepily. "I didn't know that, either."

Moments later a hand covered Toby's mouth.

A voice whispered in his ear.

"Don't say a word. Put on some warm clothes, grab that sword, and come with me."

2

Over the River and Through the Woods

They stepped quietly over sleeping Sid and headed into the closet. A faint light radiated from what should have been the back wall, but Toby knew it was the portal into *RiverHome*.

Once through the hole in the closet, he expected to feel the spray from the waterfall to his right, flowing into a stream in front of him, making its way to his left, with lush trees lining both sides of the stream.

What he did see, however, took his breath away. The waterfall had stopped falling. The stream was a dry bed of sand and rocks. The trees lining both sides of the now dry streambed were leafless. But more than that, he could feel that they were almost lifeless.

The sky was grayish. Colorless. Big dark clouds looked ready to burst. And it was cold!

He heard none of the sounds of nature that one normally expects along the stream, from birds singing to crickets cricketing—or whatever it was crickets did to make that sound.

The small footbridge that enabled them to cross the now dry stream to the walking path into *RiverHome* had crumbled. A large tree trunk served as the way over.

Toby could barely move. He could feel the pain of the land deep in his bones. Sword *Loach*—pronounced lay-uk, the Celtic word for hero, his Grandmother Baxter had told him, seemingly sensed the disease all around them, vibrating not energy, but a sense of despair.

Toby turned to his companion and realized he didn't know who his companion was. He assumed it was Deckor, but now that he thought about it, it wasn't the voice of Deckor that he had heard in his bedroom moments earlier.

His companion turned to him and pulled back his hood.

Blythar!

Blythar had been one of Clygon's lead trolls until Toby had drawn a line in the sand with the Sword at Clygon's stronghold. Blythar was one of many trolls who had left Clygon's camp, choosing peace over violence.

"Blythar." Toby held out his hand and Blythar responded by shaking it with his own.

All of the trolls that Toby had encountered the last time, smelled of sweat and vomit. Blythar, on their first meeting, was no exception. But apparently, Blythar had learned how to bathe and the touch of Old Spice... *Old Spice?*... helped. Blythar was a bit shorter than Toby, who now stood at five feet eight inches, having grown an inch since his last visit to *RiverHome.* Blythar's hair looked like straw, sticking up in every direction. His skin was rough like that of an elephant's. His nose and ears were large but his eyes were sharp. This was a warrior who didn't miss anything. He was cloaked in a dark green overcoat and carried a big axe.

"Blythar,' Toby said again, looking around him. "What's happened? Where are the river elves? Why does it feel so... so..." Words failed him.

"Come with me, Toby. There is much to tell and much to do. But we must keep moving."

Blythar led him across the dry stream using the big tree trunk bridge. Rather than heading downstream to *RiverHome,* Blythar made his way up the hill to where Toby had seen the Sword in the stone on his first adventure through his closet. His Sword, it turned out. But the trolls had managed to steal it, shattering the monument that held it, forcing Toby and the river elves on a quest to reclaim it. The empty monument had since been repaired, but the many cracks were still visible. It didn't look like it would hold much of anything.

"Quick, Toby! Put *Loach* into the stone."

"Won't I need it?"

"Not right now. *RiverHome* needs it more."

"Why? I don't understand."

"We think... we hope... that *Loach* will begin to re-energize the land... or at least give it a fighting chance."

"But Blythar, I'll be powerless... defenseless..."

"Quick, Toby! Now!"

Toby tentatively climbed onto the repaired monument. Thankfully, it held. He raised *Loach* high into the air, using both hands to steady it. He closed his eyes. He thought back to that moment when he had done the same thing at Clygon's camp—how the Sword had filled him with energy and life.

21

How he had planted the Sword in the ground, releasing an explosion that had served as a barrier of sorts between Clygon's trolls on the one side, and all those who sought peace on the other.

Loach responded to the memories. It began to vibrate, then hum. Toby found himself encircled by its glow.

Blythar stepped back and shielded his eyes.

Toby turned *Loach* so that its tip was pointed downward. He slowly slipped it into the hole in the stone and removed his hands.

Loach gave off a big burst of energy and then… fizzled. It became as gray and lifeless as the trees around it.

Toby tried to pull it out but it wouldn't budge. He tried to will energy into it but it was cold and still.

"What happened? Did I break it?"

Blythar suddenly turned his head to the left and froze for a moment.

"Run!" He grabbed Toby by the arm and pulled him off the monument and up the hill.

Once they crested the hill, they fell onto their stomachs and lifted their heads slightly, looking down toward the monument now holding *Loach*. Four trolls approached it, walking cautiously as they surveyed their surroundings.

"Plythar!" Blythar grunted.

Plythar was Blythar's brother who, unlike Blythar, had chosen to side with Clygon.

The four trolls surrounded the monument. One held an axe, the rest carried swords. Three of the trolls stood with their backs to *Loach*, watching the woods around them.

Plythar sniffed the air. "They've obviously been here," he said, nodding to the sword. "Recently, by the smell and looks of it. Stay alert!"

Plythar tentatively moved closer to *Loach*, surveying it as if searching for something. He circled around it several times, looking it up and down, including the stone monument. He slowly reached out his hand, drawing it back a few times, and finally, after several minutes, touched the sword. He let out a sigh of relief. Then laughter.

"The sword is dead, my lug-headed friends. It's cold. Lifeless. Their plan failed. It can't save them now, nor can that little boy, Toby Baxter."

The other trolls seemed to relax.

Then Plythar looked up the hill, directly at the spot where Blythar and Toby had hidden themselves. And smiled.

"Wait here," he said to the other trolls, as he made his way up the hill.

Blythar put a finger to his lips, warning Toby to remain absolutely still and quiet.

"No worries," thought Toby. But he was sure the sweat pouring from every sweat-producing pore in his body must have sounded like the waves of an ocean guiding Plythar and the trolls right to them. *How in the world do you sweat when it's freezing cold?*

Blythar quickly rolled onto his back, his axe at the ready. Toby, just as quickly, shimmied behind a large tree three feet away.

The waiting seemed interminable. *Interminable? Now's not the time for big words, Author!*

They heard a twig snap, indicating Plythar was close. And then… nothing. And then… more nothing. Followed by more… nothing.

"My brother, Blythar, has been here. I can sense him. He's got the boy with him."

Plythar must have been ten feet from them, just below the crest of the hill. Toby held back a gag as the smell of sweat and vomit wafted over him, times four. Surely Plythar could hear the thumping of Toby's racing heart! He could see Blythar, tense and ready to attack.

"If that makeshift sword is dead," shouted one of the trolls, "and their plan has failed, let's move on. They have nowhere to go and we should get back to camp before sundown."

"Hang on! Can you imagine the riches Clygon will give us and the glory we'll receive if we bring that traitor Blythar and the kid to him? We'll be set up for life. I say we find them." This from one of the other trolls.

From a distance, a loud horn sounded out.

"The camp is calling. We best obey," said Plythar.

Another moment of quiet as the trolls decided what to do. The cracking of twigs suggested that they were headed down to the path.

Just as Toby was about to relax, a small stone landed next to Blythar. He quietly picked it up and stared at it.

After a few more moments of holding his breath, Toby let out a sigh of relief. He quickly jumped to his feet, unzipped his pants and relieved himself. Another minute or two and he'd have wet his pants.

Blythar was no longer poised for an attack. But he continued to lay—*or is it… Nope! I'm on winter break. And that means a break from grammar, Author!*—on his back, his axe on his chest. Slowly, at first, a rumble, starting

23

from deep in his soul, turned into a loud, joy-filled laugh. He jumped to his feet and slapped Toby on his shoulder, a bit too hard for Toby's liking.

Maybe this was the way Blythar relieved stress, something like what Toby did by peeing by the tree.

Blythar put his arm around Toby and said, "For one small moment in this hopeless world, a glimmer of hope, my friend, Toby."

"What are you talking about, Blythar? We were seconds away from being Clygon's captives, or worse."

"Here, my young friend. Look at this." Blythar showed him the small stone. It was the shape of an egg with an E carved into the middle of it.

"What is it?" Toby asked.

"This is an Esther Egg!"

"An Easter Egg?"

"No, an Esther Egg."

"What does it mean?"'

"The Esther Egg is the sign of the Resistance against Clygon. It's based on an ancient story about a Jewish woman named Esther, who was chosen to be the wife of a Persian King. The King was tricked into issuing a decree to have all of Esther's people—the Jews—killed. The only one who could save them was Esther. To do so meant she had to put her own life at risk. But she stepped into the moment and her people were spared."

Toby remembered the story from Sunday school.

"This small stone is one of the ways we identify who's a part of the Resistance," Blythar went on.

"But what if Plythar got a hold of one of those Esther Eggs and is using it to trick you?"

"It's a good question, Toby Baxter. But see this small mark here?"

Toby looked closely. The mark was barely noticeable.

"That's a symbol only Plythar and I share together. It's a sign that we always have each other's back."

"Um… okay…"

"Don't you get it, Toby? He knew we were here all along. He didn't turn us in. Instead, he threw this stone to let me know that he's on our side. He must be working as a spy inside Clygon's camp. My brother… is on our side!"

Toby thought Blythar was delusional but he seemed so happy that Toby didn't want to ruin the moment.

Then Blythar grabbed Toby by the arm.

"Look at your hands!"

Toby's hands were glowing.

"Quickly, to *Loach!"* Blythar shouted.

He led Toby down the hill to the monument.

"Jump up on the stone and put your hands on the sword!"

"Why? It's dead. It's useless."

"Just do it!" barked Blythar.

Toby did as ordered and put both hands onto the hilt of *Loach*. Instantly, he felt an explosion of power filling his whole body. He, once again, saw himself in Clygon's stronghold, planting the Sword into the ground, drawing a line in the sand between peace and violence.

Then he saw… his father. He was Toby's age. He watched as his father raised the Sword toward the sky, energy flowing out of him to the river elves, Clovor, Phoenix, Deckor, Judah, and Mathilda, as they fought off trolls.

Next, he saw… his Grandpa Baxter, again, about the same age as Toby. It must have been him although he had died when Toby was a little boy. Grandpa Baxter stood with the Sword held high in the middle of a battle with the trolls, glowing and radiating power.

Finally, he saw… his Great-grandpa Baxter. He, too, about thirteen-years-old, was holding the Sword toward the sky. He, too, radiated power as he stood high on a hill. The fighting below him was fierce but the Sword seemed to inspire the river elf warriors.

The power surging through Toby was so intense that he felt he was about to explode. He opened his eyes and peeled his hands off of the hilt. The energy inside of him slowly dissipated but *Loach* continued to glow. Not brightly, but just enough to suggest that it wasn't as lifeless as it had seemed.

"Good. Now, let's get out of here," Blythar said.

Rather than heading down the hill and taking the path along the stream to *RiverHome,* Blythar led him back up the hill, through the woods, taking an alternate route to their destination.

"Blythar. Please. What's going on? Where is everyone? Why does everything seem so lifeless?"

Blythar stopped and faced him.

"Because, Toby, we've lost hope!"

"How? What happened? What's so awful that you would all give up on hope?"

"That's not what I mean, Toby. We've lost hope. Clygon has it. Clygon has the giant."

3

To Grandmother's House We Go

"What? How? When did this happen? Is this why I'm here?"

Before Blythar could answer, they rounded the corner to *RiverHome*. Toby had never seen *RiverHome* from this perspective, standing above it. He could see the playing field across the dry streambed, the grass dead and the bleachers badly in need of repair. Many of the entryways into the elves' homes carved into the cliff walls were boarded up. The place seemed completely empty. It felt dead.

Blythar nudged him to his right and they headed down a hard-to-see path that eventually led them to a hidden entrance. Blythar made a coded knock on the door.

"Where are we?" asked Toby.

A coded knock responded to them from the inside. Blythar replied with yet another coded knock. A moment later, the door opened and Blythar led Toby down a dark corridor. Toby couldn't see a thing but Blythar knew exactly where he was going. The path took them down a slope followed by dozens of steps, leading them deeper and deeper underground. Toby started to feel claustrophobic. He began to sweat. He needed to get out. But just before he turned to run back up the steps to fresh air, he was met by a warm amber light reaching out to them at the bottom of the stairs.

And he could smell freshly baked bread and roasted sweet potatoes. And something else. Chocolate. Deep, rich, enticing chocolate.

They reached the bottom of the stairs and a river elf sentinel saluted Blythar and Toby by raising his right fist to his left chest. He led them into a huge hall where they were immediately met by an explosion of activity.

Around a huge, round table stood Donold, the captain of the river elf army, along with twenty river elf troops, poring over a large map. Running back and forth behind and around them, were more elves scurrying about with papers and other forms of what Toby guessed were intel. *Is that the word?* Several drones, their human heads on their big bird bodies, chattered back and forth. Off to his right, Toby saw the source of the delicious aromas; a food table being set by an elderly elven woman.

She turned and spotted Toby.

"Toby!" she said. Not loudly. Her voice was weak. Yet commanding enough for the entire room to stop and look at him and Blythar. Instantly, every river elf soldier stood to attention and saluted Toby.

The elderly woman picked up a walking stick and hobbled her way over to Toby and threw her arms around him.

"Grandma?" Toby was dismayed at her appearance. She had been so alive... so strong the last time he had seen her. Now her long braided hair was fully gray, her thin body hunched over as if no longer strong enough to stand up straight, and her skin almost see-through.

Donold walked over and grabbed Toby's hand and shook it. He did the same with Blythar.

"Toby," Donold nodded in greeting.

"Blythar." Another nod from Donold.

"You are well met. I wish it were under better circumstances. As you can see..."

"Not now, Donold," Grandma interrupted. "There will be plenty of time to get caught up. Since our guest of honor is here, now is a good time to take a break and have something to eat. The food is ready."

"Thank you, Blythar," she whispered, "for bringing him here."

Grandma brushed Donold out of the way, grabbed Toby by the arm and dragged him to the food table. The woman still had chutzpah! *He'd have to look that word up later.*

The smell of the food, as always, was mouth-watering. But the spread of the food was a shock. Toby was used to a bounty of food from breads to sweet potatoes to roasted vegetables to succulent desserts to the energizing river elf drink. This table was sparse in comparison. The breads were cut into small pieces to make the breadbasket look fuller than it actually was. Same with the sweet potatoes. Off to the side—water. Fresh, clean water. But poured out sparingly. The chocolate smell came from a small cup of what looked like hot sipping chocolate, with a sign that read, 'For Toby only!'

Toby was starving. Normally in *RiverHome,* he could eat until his stomach was ready to explode. But this table of food couldn't possibly feed all of them unless each of them stuck to a very small amount.

He looked around at everyone and realized how gaunt they all appeared. Donold had lost a lot of weight, even though he was still an imposing character, albeit still a good seven inches shorter than Toby. The river elves were similar in size to Santa's elves from the old stop-motion Rudolph the Red-Nosed Reindeer TV show. Come to think of it, Blythar seemed to have lost weight as well.

Grandma shushed them all and had them form a circle, joining hands. They began to hum, that now familiar Celtic-music-type hum that always filled Toby with a renewed sense of energy. As it did now.

Grandma started to pray, "O, Creator of this bounty, we give you thanks today for bringing our friend, Toby, back to us. We praise you for your care…"

But then Grandma went silent. Toby looked at her and saw that she was weeping.

The circle broke and some headed quietly to the table to grab a small piece of bread or sweet potato. Donold walked over to Grandma, put his arm around her frail shoulders, and led her to a side room.

Toby turned to Blythar and mouthed, "What's happened?"

"I can answer that, Toby Baxter."

Toby turned to the voice. He recognized it but not the person behind it. Clovor?

She looked like a river elf who had lost all hope.

4

Let it Snow

Sid woke up, not sure at first where he was. Light was trickling in through the edges of the window shade so he knew it was morning. It took a minute but his brain computed that he was on the floor in Toby's bedroom. The last thing he remembered from the night before, was mentioning to Toby that the sword on the wall was glowing.

He looked up and saw that the sword was no longer there. He also noticed that Toby wasn't in bed.

Sid got up, threw on a pair of pants and a sweatshirt, and opened the door leading into the kitchen. The smell of bacon hit him immediately.

"I thought you boys might be hungry," Thomas, his back to Sid, said as he flipped over a couple of pancakes. "Especially after that tough loss for your Vikes last night."

"You don't need to rub it in, Mr B," Sid responded as he scratched his nose and wiped the bacon-induced drool from his chin.

"Did you sleep well on the floor?"

"I was out like a light."

Sid turned toward the kitchen window to see that it was snowing. Another big, heavy snow. It was turning out to be a fantastic winter break. Lots of snow piling up just in time for Christmas. And for more sledding down Toby's roof.

Thomas lifted some bacon off of the frying pan and put it onto a plate.

"Is Toby still sleeping?"

"Ah… I don't think so. I thought he would be out here. He wasn't in bed."

Thomas turned and stared at Sid.

"Maybe he's in the bathroom?" Sid suggested.

Something about Thomas made him suddenly feel anxious. Thomas ran through Toby's bedroom and out the other door into the hallway. The bathroom was empty.

"Toby? Toby?" Thomas made his way through the house, down into the basement, and back up again.

"I noticed that the sword hanging on his wall is missing, if that helps," Sid said.

Thomas stopped. He pulled up a chair to the kitchen table and sat down.

"Sid, this is really important. Tell me exactly what happened last night when you went to bed."

"Nothing really. We talked about the game a bit. Then I noticed the sword was glowing and said something about it..."

"The sword was glowing?"

"Yah, I'd never seen it do that before."

Sid watched as Thomas stared out the window. Then, Thomas began to massage a strange-looking green line from the wrist to the knuckle on his right hand. Toby had one just like it.

"Did you hear anything? Did you sense anything?" The questions betrayed a sense of urgency.

"Mr B, you're making me really nervous. Is something wrong? Did something happen to Toby?"

Thomas got up and headed back into Toby's bedroom. Sid turned and watched as Thomas opened the closet door and stared into the closet for several moments.

Was it his imagination, or did he see flurries of snow coming out of the closet? Did the Baxters have a hole in the roof?

Thomas returned to the kitchen and sat down. He looked like he was struggling with a decision. After a few moments of silence, he stood up.

"Sid, I need you to trust me. Are you up for an adventure?"

"Um... sure... I guess. What kind of adventure?"

"The kind that will call forth the HERO in you."

Sid had no idea what to make of that but followed Thomas back into Toby's bedroom. He watched as Thomas opened the closet door once again. And once again, Sid swore he could see snow flurries coming out of the closet. This time he also felt a blast of cold air. There had to be a hole in the roof.

Thomas shut the closet door and turned to Sid. Sid could tell he was lost in thought.

"Okay, Sid. Let's do this. Can you get your winter coat, your stocking cap, and your boots and meet me back here in five minutes? You might want to use the bathroom first."

Sid grew increasingly concerned about Mr B's strange behavior. But he also sensed something big was about to happen.

After using the bathroom, he threw on his coat, his cap, and his boots and found Thomas in Toby's bedroom. He, too, had his warm winter clothes on.

"Okay, Sid. Okay… okay… okay… um… okay. I'm going to open this closet door and I want you to stay close. Keep your eyes on my back. I don't want to lose you."

Sid thought Thomas was losing his marbles. *How could he get lost in a closet?*

But then, Thomas opened the closet door. They were met with a blast of cold wind and snow flurries… coming from what should have been the back wall of the closet!

Sid followed Thomas into the closet… and out into the cold.

5

In the Bleak Midwinter

Clovor walked over to Toby and gave him a hug, her head coming up to his chest. He could almost feel her bones through her leather winter coat. He could sense tears starting to tickle his eyes as he took in the sense of loss and pain all around him.

"Sit down, Friend Toby." Clovor pointed to a couple of chairs by the food table. "Have something to eat."

Toby put a couple of small sweet potato cubes onto his plate. But as hungry as he was, he wasn't in the mood to eat.

Clovor sat next to him. Her dark brown hair held traces of gray. Small bags hung out under her eyes—metaphorically, not literally. Although they did look like bags under her eyes. But those deep, brown eyes still had spirit in them.

The others went back to whatever business they were about before Toby arrived.

Clovor leaned back, closed her eyes for a moment, and let out a big sigh.

"Where are the others?" Toby asked. "Phoenix, Deckor, Judah, and Mathilda?"

"Around," Clovor responded vaguely, her eyes still closed.

"How long have I been gone?"

"Two of your years, maybe? Remember, time in our world works differently than it does in your world."

"Two years?" Toby said. *It's only been a few months, hasn't it?*

The two of them sat silently together, Toby waiting for Clovor to tell the story when she was ready.

Then a familiar voice rang through the hall.

"Where is he? Where's Toby?"

Before he could answer, Mathilda dived at him, knocking him off the chair onto the hard floor, her furry winter coat almost suffocating him. After

33

a big bear hug, she rolled off of him, jumped to her feet, and pulled him back onto his. She, too, looked thin, but she'd lost none of her energy or enthusiasm.

Mathilda's entrance seemed to bring a bit of life into the gloomy, serious hall.

She pulled up a chair next to Toby. She looked from him to Clovor and back to Toby.

"You haven't told him yet?" Her question was directed to Clovor.

"I was just about to when you flew in. Thankfully! It will be much easier with you. I'm afraid I'm not at my best today."

Donold asked for everyone's attention. Blythar quickly explained to the room what had happened at the monument when Toby put *Loach* into the Sword's slot and how life began to flow from it. Everyone cheered. A small, but significant victory. He also showed them the Esther Egg Plythar had tossed their way, indicating that Plythar was working on their behalf. That news, Toby sensed, was met with skepticism.

When Blythar was done, Toby turned to Clovor and Mathilda.

"Blythar said you've lost Christmas?"

"Technically," Mathilda said, "we didn't lose Christmas. You can't lose Christmas. We lost the Christmas Giant. And again, we didn't really lose him. Clygon took him, we think."

"You think?"

"We aren't sure if Clygon captured him or if the Christmas Giant willingly gave himself up to the trolls."

"Why would he do such a thing?"

"Perhaps we should start at the beginning," Clovor said.

Suddenly Toby felt the need to hum. As he did, Clovor and Mathilda stared at him.

"What are you humming Toby?" Mathilda asked.

"Sorry, when Clovor said we should start at the beginning, a song from my Grandma Baxter's favorite movie, *The Sound of Music,* popped into my head."

"Oh, is that the one with the seventy-six trombones?"

"No, that's from *The Music Man.*"

"I'm more of a *Wicked* girl myself," giggled Mathilda.

Suddenly, Toby and Mathilda looked at each other, and then together, turned to Clovor.

"Clovor, I am so sorry. We didn't mean to be flippant," Mathilda said.

34

Clovor smiled. It was the first smile since she had walked into the room. "My all-time favorite is *Les Misérables.*"

"It is so good to have you back with us, Toby. You give us hope. And Mathilda, you keep me balanced."

She leaned back into her chair and closed her eyes again but kept on smiling, perhaps humming a song from *Les Misérables* to herself.

After a few moments, she opened her eyes, sat up, clapped her hands, and said, "Okay, let's get at this.

"Toby, after you left us and went back home, life here returned to normal. The dynamics had changed a bit as we now had refugees from Clygon's camp moving in nearby. But united by our common will to keep the peace, we learned to appreciate our differences. We even created some new footy teams. Blythar and his friends called their team the Lions, and if it weren't for a heroic kick by Deckor at the end of regulation, the Lions would have been last year's champs.

"We knew that the barrier you created with the Sword wouldn't last forever, but we didn't anticipate that it would fail us so soon. We still aren't quite sure how the energy field collapsed, but our first realization of trouble came when we heard that horrific battle cry of Clygon once again. I had forgotten just how bone-chilling it is."

"Wait a minute," Toby said. "My dad and I heard Clygon in our world. I wonder if it was around the same time? He said something about having a friend of mine. Do you think he meant the giant? But for me, that was just a day or two ago…"

"For us," Clovor continued," it was many, many months ago. And much has happened in that time."

"It's a…" Mathilda began.

"I know. It's a timey-wimey thing," Toby said.

6

Do You Hear What I Hear?

Sid stopped and stared. His mouth wide open. In front of him, he saw a dry streambed that had apparently been fed by a now waterless waterfall to his right. A tree trunk over the streambed led to a path on the other side, which ran along the dry stream to his left.

Just above the path, up the hill, he could see something shining. It looked like... *a sword? Was that... Toby's sword?*

He turned back to the closet but saw only a stone wall reaching high above him. Heavy, wet snow was falling onto his face. Thankfully, Mr B had told him to dress warm because it was cold!

As he tried to get his bearings, he had the growing sense that something about the place looked familiar. He'd been here before, or somewhere that looked a lot like it. He just about had it...

"Sid... Sid!" Thomas grabbed him by the arm.

"Where are we?" Sid asked.

"There's no time for that. Something is terribly wrong. We need to move. We need to get to *RiverHome.*"

"River what?"

But Thomas was already scrambling over the tree trunk. Sid quickly chased after him, and just as he reached the other side of the dry stream, he was assaulted by the creepiest laughter he had ever heard. Followed by what could only be described as shrieking.

THOMAS BAXTER. HOW GOOD OF YOU TO COME! AND YOU'VE BROUGHT A FRIEND ALONG. THE MORE, THE MERRIER! CAN YOU FEEL IT, THOMAS? HOPE IS GONE. AND NEITHER YOU NOR TOBY NOR THAT YOUNG FRIEND OF YOURS CAN HELP. GO HOME, THOMAS. THERE'S NOTHING FOR YOU HERE!

More creepy laughter.

Sid stood still. Unable to move. Unable to think straight. Trying hard not to pee his pants… or worse.

"Sid…! Come on! We have to keep moving."

"Did you hear it, Mr B? What was that? Who was that? And how did it know we were here? How did it know your name? Is Toby here?"

The words poured out of him in the form of one big sentence.

Thomas put his hands on Sid's shoulders and looked him in the eyes.

"Sid, look at me. Take a deep breath and look at me. I heard it. I'll explain everything as soon as I can, but right now, you need to trust me. You need to follow me. We need to get to *RiverHome*. It's just downstream from here. Can you do that, Sid?"

Without waiting for an answer Thomas turned, grabbed Sid by the arm, and dragged him down the stream path.

Moments later the path opened up. To his left, on the other side of the stream, Sid noticed an open space. Perhaps a playing field of some sort. Hard to tell with the growing snowstorm.

In the cliff walls to his right, he saw boarded-up holes with small paths leading to them. The dry stream continued on in front of them.

Thomas stopped. He put a finger to his lips warning Sid to be quiet.

"The place seems to be abandoned," Thomas said more to himself than to Sid.

Thomas looked around, wondering what to do next when they both heard a twig snap behind them.

Sid suddenly smelled a noxious scent of sweat and vomit, felt something sharp against his back, and heard a voice whisper in his ear.

"Don't move!"

***

Phoenix and Deckor looked down onto the dry streambed from a protected perch above one of the *RiverHome* cliff walls. They watched as a man and a boy about Toby Baxter's age slowly made their way along the path. They saw four trolls stealthily surround the two of them, one of them, the leader, pointing a sword into the back of the boy.

"That's Thomas Baxter!" Deckor whispered a bit too loudly to Phoenix. One of the trolls turned and looked up in their direction.

"And that's Plythar, Blythar's brother," said Phoenix. "How did we not know trolls were in *RiverHome*? And what's Thomas Baxter doing here? Who's that boy with him? And what are we going to do?"

***

Sid could see three hairy, rough-skinned something-or-others out of the corners of his eyes and knew about the fourth since something sharp—*a sword?*—was toying with his back. The smell was overwhelming as was Sid's sense of fear.

"Well, well, well. Who do we have here?" The one with the sword, obviously the leader, moved around to face both Thomas and Sid.

The person—*what is he or it exactly?*—stood a bit shorter than Sid. It wore some sort of animal skin with buff arms exposed. Hair—*or is that straw?*—grew out of its oversized ears and elbows, its skin rough like that of a rhino's. The cold didn't seem to bother it. Frozen mist-like fractals all around came out of its huge nostrils as it breathed. In some ways, it reminded Sid of the gridiron warriors of the NFL at one of those December games in Denver or New York.

Sid noticed Mr B's eyes widened a bit as he seemed to recognize whatever or whoever was standing in front of them.

"Ah, Thomas Baxter! I see you remember me." Its voice was low and gravelly. "So good to see you again," he sneered. "How long has it been? Over twenty-five of your years now, is it?"

Your years? What is this place? And what is this beast... this thing... this person in front of us and how does he know Mr B? And what is that horrific smell?

Sid wanted to run. He wanted to wake up. He wanted to puke! But he kept his eyes on Mr B who seemed to be in a staring contest with whatever that thing was talking to him.

He noticed one of the others turn and look up at one of the cliffs above.

"You'll be happy to know your son is here… somewhere… not far from here. We'll find him, no doubt about that. And then, we'll take the two of you, father and son, to get reacquainted with your friend, Clygon."

The malice with which he said Clygon sent shivers up and down Sid's spine.

"And I see you brought a friend along, or, just a guess, a friend of Toby's?"

38

The sword moved up to Sid's neck. Thomas flinched.

"Plythar!" Thomas Baxter said, more a command than a statement.

This thing has a name?

Calmly, and yet with a certain amount of danger in his voice, Mr B said, "This is Sid. And you're right. He's a friend of Toby's. It was a mistake to bring him here. He has nothing to do with this. Let him go back through the portal."

Were Mr B's hands glowing slightly?

"I'm afraid that's just not possible, sadly, Thomas. But I promise you we will treat Sid with the same courtesy we will extend to you and your little boy."

Plythar laughed. A terrifying, sweat-inducing laugh.

Plythar turned his attention to Sid.

"I can see you're confused, my new friend. My name is Plythar, as you've heard. We're trolls."

"Trolls?" Sid croaked out. "You don't look anything like the trolls from those Justin Bieber animated films." He regretted the words as soon as they came out of his mouth.

Plythar moved the sword an inch closer to Sid's neck.

"No. We don't!"

Sid almost fell backwards at the force of Plythar's anger.

"And it was Justin Timberlake, not Justin Bieber," the troll said.

***

"We need to do something—now—before Plythar lops that boy's head off!"

Phoenix was about to jump over the ledge when Deckor stopped him.

"Give it another minute. We need to make sure it's just the four trolls."

***

"Tie them up!" Plythar shouted at one of the trolls.

Rough, sandpaper-like hands forced Sid's arms behind his back and tied his hands together. The same happened to Thomas.

A horn sounded in the distance.

"You three dunderheads," Plythar shouted at the trolls, "head down the stream. I'll meet you there. I'd like a moment alone with Thomas Baxter and our new friend, Sid."

The look of evil humor on Plythar's face caused the other three trolls to laugh as they headed off down the path.

Sid, on the other hand, was sure he was about to empty all of his bodily fluids into his pants.

***

Plythar looked up toward the cliff wall and smiled.

"Now!"

Sid heard the shout coming from behind him and turned to see what Plythar was smiling at.

Two—*people?*... he couldn't quite tell... leaped over the edge of the cliff and slid down the wall toward them, their swords at the ready.

Plythar dropped his weapon and put up his hands, a smirk crossing his troll face.

"Don't move!" one of the newcomers demanded.

"I have no intention of moving."

Sid found himself staring at two grown men who were about six to seven inches shorter than he was. They had pointy ears and their eyebrows looked like those of Mr Spock from *Star Trek*. Both had curly brown hair and dark brown eyes. *Brothers maybe?* Their feet were large and hairy. *Hobbits?* One of them wore an Arizona Cardinals stocking cap and the other a vintage Minnesota Vikings parka that had seen better days.

"I don't have much time," Plythar said.

He handed the Vikings hobbit a small rock shaped like an egg.

"An Esther Egg?" the Cardinals hobbit asked. "I don't understand? Are you a part of the Resistance?"

Resistance? This is getting weirder by the second.

Plythar nodded.

"Clygon doesn't suspect a thing. Let's keep it that way. One of you needs to bean me on the head with the butt of your sword."

"Gladly!" both hobbits said at the same time.

"But before you do, bring this message to Donold: *Ogreton Heights.* That's where you'll find hope. The trolls have hired ogre mercenaries. You have no idea how outnumbered you are. Then, again, there's a new sword in town. Toby is back. Thomas is back. And Sid is here... for some reason. Now, hit me on the noggin and get out of here."

40

The Vikings hobbit lifted his sword and butted Plythar on the head. But Sid couldn't tell who was hurt worse—Plythar or the hobbit. Plythar wobbled a bit. But the hobbit literally shivered like a cartoon character who had been sandwiched between two cymbals.

"Go! Plythar shouted as he fell to the ground.

7

Chestnuts Roasting on an Open Fire

Vikings hobbit quickly cut the bands around Sid's wrists while Cardinals hobbit did the same for Thomas. Thomas nodded at Sid to follow the hobbits as they made their way back up the cliff wall path from where the hobbits had first appeared. They passed several of those boarded-up doors Sid had seen earlier... *entrances to hobbit homes?*

"What's happened here?" Thomas asked.

"We'll fill you in later. Right now, we need to hide before those trolls come back," Vikings hobbit said.

Reaching the top of the cliff, they ducked behind a large rock. Then the four of them slowly raised their heads and looked down below.

Sure enough, two of the trolls returned, only to find Plythar out cold. Apparently, Plythar was a good actor. Once they revived him, the trolls and Plythar engaged in what appeared to be a heated conversation. Plythar pointed toward the increasingly snow-covered playing field across the increasingly snow-covered dry streambed, sending the trolls off in the wrong direction. As the trolls huffed away, Plythar looked up the cliff, gave a slight nod, and then made his way down the streambed path.

The two hobbits turned around and slumped down with their backs against the cliff wall. Sid and Thomas did the same.

"What's this about ogre mercenaries?" Vikings asked Cardinals.

"First I'm hearing of it," Cardinals said.

"Aren't the ogres neutral when it comes to conflicts between the trolls and their enemies?" Thomas asked.

"Like Finland in your world," Vikings said.

"Not Finland. Norway," Cardinals corrected.

"It's Switzerland," Sid chimed in.

Vikings noticed Sid staring at his parka.

"Vintage Vikings. 1970s. The Super… um… ah… the Big Game years for the Vikings," he explained.

"The Big Game?" Sid asked. "Do you mean the Sup…"

Vikings put his hand on Sid's mouth, looking around nervously.

"Never mind him. I'm Deckor," said Cardinals. "This is my sometimes-weird brother, Phoenix."

"Are you… hobbits?" Sid asked, pointing at their feet.

"I asked that same question my first time here," Thomas laughed.

"So did Toby. But no. We're not hobbits, although we like to pretend that we are distant relatives. We're river elves. Below you is *RiverHome*. And these are boots, not our feet," Deckor said.

"O… kay… well… I'm Sid. A human. Currently living in Minneapolis on planet Earth."

Phoenix laughed and slapped Sid on his shoulder. "Well met, Friend Sid."

"Thomas. It's good to see you again. But why are you here?" Deckor asked.

"Toby came here last night."

"Last night?" Phoenix said. "Is that what Plythar was talking about when he said Toby is back?"

Deckor could see the confusion on Thomas's face.

"We haven't seen him."

"Wait a minute, Deckor. We felt that very slight change in the land several hours ago. Thomas, did Toby bring *Loach*? Plythar said something about a new sword in town…"

"Only hours ago?" Thomas asked. "I was afraid it would have been a week ago or more by now in *RiverHome* time?"

"It might have been, but everything is off since the force-field collapsed," Deckor explained.

Phoenix whispered to Sid. "It's a timey-wimey thing,"

Elves. Trolls. Ogres. RiverHome. And now Doctor Who references. Where am I?

"Yes, he brought it. But if you didn't know he was here, where could he be?" Thomas asked, a hint of desperation in his voice.

"Look, Toby has already proven himself a HERO, just like you did, Thomas…" Phoenix said.

"I think it's *just as* you did," Deckor interrupted.

"Nope. Pretty sure it's like. What do you think, Sid?"

43

"I vote like," Sid replied.

"Anyway, let's not quibble about grammar right now," said Phoenix. "Nice word, by the way, quibble! Not quite as good as indubitably but still, a good word. My point is that he can take care of himself. Let's get you to Command Central. No doubt Toby is there as we speak."

"Command Central?" asked Thomas as Deckor helped him to his feet.

"We've had to move underground away from the prying eyes of Clygon. Follow us."

The river elves led Thomas and Sid higher up the rocky hill. The snow was falling hard now. It was getting difficult to see, but the two elves knew where they were headed.

Phoenix suddenly stopped and put a finger to his lips.

"Something's wrong," he whispered.

He pointed to what looked like an entrance into the side of a hill.

"This door shouldn't be open."

The two elves drew out their swords and told Thomas and Sid to follow quietly. Before they moved, Sid pointed to a bright blue object on the ground. It looked like an Easter Egg.

Deckor picked it up. He rolled it in his fingers. He smelled it.

"It's an Eogre Egg."

"An Ogre Egg?" Sid asked.

"An Eogre Egg. The E is silent," Phoenix clarified.

"How am I supposed to know there's a silent E if the E is silent? And if the E is silent, why have it there at all?" Sid asked.

Phoenix and Deckor simply stared at him.

"The ogres have created a way for their chickens to produce colorful, high-energy eggs," Deckor continued. "Some of the most delicious eggs you'll find in this world. But something is off about this one."

Phoenix pointed to a bright red egg a few feet away. And then to a multi-colored one to his right. Then he nodded to the door.

The two elves cautiously pushed the door the rest of the way open and slowly began to descend the path, and then, several flights of stairs, with Thomas and Sid behind them. A warm glow radiated up from the bottom of the stairs, but other than that, all was quiet.

When they reached the bottom of the stairs, Phoenix gasped. River elves lay passed out all over the floor, half-eaten Eogre eggs all around them.

Scurrying around were what Sid could only describe as lawn gnomes, caring for the elves and feeding them some kind of nut that appeared to help them wake up.

They heard a groan off to their left.

"Donold!" Deckor said.

The river elf called Donold slowly climbed onto his knees and then, using a table to steady himself, stood to his feet. Others began to move as well.

Phoenix ran over to Donold and walked him to a chair.

"Donold! What happened?"

"I'll tell you."

The female voice came from a fireplace.

She looked like a female version of a lawn gnome, nuts roasting on top of the fire next to her.

"Roxie!" Phoenix shouted as he ran to her, picked her up in his arms, and kissed her.

"They've taken Toby. And Clovor."

"Who?" Thomas asked. "Who took Toby?

"Ogres."

Roxie buried her face in Phoenix's shoulder and wept.

8

Sleigh Ride

Toby tried to open his eyes. His brain was mush. His head hurt. His body ached. *What hit me?*

He vaguely remembered what had happened. One of the elves had come into the Command Center carrying a basket of what looked like Easter eggs. Mathilda told him they were Eogre Eggs—the E, by the way, being silent. *If the E is silent, why is it there?* The ogres had apparently figured out how to engineer eggs in such a way that they came out in a variety of colors and boasted a days' worth of vitamins and protein.

The last thing he remembered was taking a bite of a multi-colored egg.

He heard someone groaning next to him. Clovor! She slowly opened her eyes and looked at him. She seemed as mushy-brained as he felt.

He realized then that he was cold. Icey wind ripped through his clothes and the blanket—*how did that get there?*—covering part of his body. He looked up and saw that he was outside, moving up a snow-covered mountain… in a sleigh.

From the back, through his mush-brain eyes, the driver of the sleigh looked like Thor from the Marvel movies. His ripped bare arms were red from the cold. His long blond hair, under… *a Santa hat?*… flowed behind him.

Who played him in the movies? Robert Downey, Jr?… no… Michael Keaton?… no… Chris something… that's it… Chris Pine?… no, that's not it… Chris Pratt?… yah, that's… no, that's not… Chris Evans…

"Chris Helmsworth," Clovor whispered.

"How do you do that?

"Do what?"

"Read my thoughts?"

"I didn't read your thoughts. I was asking myself the same question and guessed you were too. I just got to the answer faster." Clovor shook her head trying to remove the cobwebs.

46

Sensing they were looking at him, the driver turned and flashed a small grin. To Toby's surprise, the face didn't match the rest of his body. His eyes were small and too close together. His nose, if that's what that thing was under his eyes, was overly big for the face, rippled with blood vessels. His lips, purple from the cold, were two thin lines. His beard was splotchy at best. And his ears looked like they had been in far too many boxing matches—gnarled and scarred.

Toby looked at Clovor.

"He's an ogre," she whispered.

"The name's Oreeo. At your service, young master Baxter and small elven woman."

The voice was scratchy and harsh sounding.

"Oreo?" Toby asked. "Like the cookie?"

"Or-EE-o," the ogre shouted.

Toby was about to ask another question when Oreeo yelled out, "On, Hermey! On, Philly! On, Rayfa!" followed by the lash of a whip.

Hermey? Philly? Rayfa?

Toby looked up front, and to his horror, saw three beautiful unicorns pulling the sleigh. He had met them his last day in *RiverHome* on his first visit.

Oreeo turned to Toby and Clovor with a grin. "As you can see, we have recaptured what you elves stole from us all those years ago, and even added one!" He turned back to the unicorns, laughing and lashing them with his whip.

Now Toby was fully awake. And he was livid. He hadn't been this angry since his showdown with Clygon, the moment Mathilda had been thrown, broken and almost lifeless, onto the ground before him. He could feel energy filling him. He saw that his hands were starting to glow bright red. He was about to lose control. But this time, he didn't have the Sword.

Clovor touched his arm.

"Look at me, Toby. Take a deep breath. Now, take another. Remember, you're no good to us when you're out of control."

Slowly the anger died down.

"He's going to pay for this," he muttered under his breath.

He pulled the blanket over his body to try to get some warmth.

"What happened to us?" he asked Clovor. "How did we end up in this sleigh and where are we going?"

It was Oreeo who answered. His ears may be disgusting-looking, but apparently, his hearing was spot on. *Spot on? Author's handiwork again, no doubt.*

"You had the pleasure of eating one of our Eogre Sleeping Eggs. The E is silent, in case you were wondering. Beats melatonin every time! And before you ask, we're headed to *Ogreton Heights*. I can't say much, but we have a surprise planned for you there."

"The ogres have always been neutral in our clashes with the trolls and even friendly toward us, despite some of our... um... disagreements." She nodded toward the unicorns. "I sense that has changed?" Clovor said.

Oreeo gave her one of his thin smiles. "You sense correctly, small elf woman. Clygon offered us a deal we couldn't refuse."

Oreeo picked up his whip and moved his arm back. But just as he was about to lash the unicorns, Toby yanked the whip out of his hand and tossed it out of the sleigh.

Oreeo turned on him. His small beady eyes enraged. He dropped the reigns and stood up, his fist ready to knock Toby's head off, literally, not metaphorically.

Toby stood to face him, fighting back his anger with a smile, his hands held up as a form of surrender.

"Give me a chance to explain myself, Mr Oreeo, sir. I know these unicorns. I think I can encourage them to get us to wherever you are taking us without the whip."

Oreeo stared down Toby, until a bump in the path knocked Oreeo back onto his seat.

"Okay, young master Baxter. But no funny stuff or I'll rip that horn off of Rayfa's head."

Toby saw Rayfa turn to him. He could have sworn Rayfa was pleading with him to behave himself.

Toby slowly moved his way past Oreeo to the front of the sleigh. Snow was falling, and with the darkening sky, it was hard to see the path below. Thankfully, the unicorns had extraordinary vision.

"Rayfa, Hermey, Philly," he yelled. "I won't let him hurt you. Just get us to wherever it is we are going and we'll let you rest. I promise. Right, Mr Oreeo?"

The unicorns slowed their pace as it became almost impossible to see through the snow. The torch lamps on the sleigh, though bright, didn't help.

Toby moved past Oreeo on his way back to Clovor. He sat on the bench, snuggled up next to her for warmth, and repositioned the blanket over them.

They sat huddled together—the sleigh skis slicing through the snow, the snorting of the unicorns and the wind the only sounds they heard.

Toby felt himself nodding off when his head fell to his chest, then bounced back up, startling him. Clovor laughed at him.

He looked at her. Her face was so weary. He could feel her anxiety.

"Why does everything seem so gray… so lifeless… so dead?"

Clovor sighed. "It has to do with the Sword."

"I'm guessing you didn't tell me everything about the Sword the last time I was here?"

"Very perceptive, Toby. You're right. Not all of it, no. But we told you what you needed for that moment."

Clovor shifted so that she could face Toby and lower her voice.

"The Sword not only serves to protect us but it also feeds energy into the land. We knew that, after you planted the Sword in the ground, at some point, the Sword's force field would eventually lose its power. But we never, ever thought that the Sword would lose its ability to nourish the land. This has never happened before."

"What do you think happened?"

"Our best guess? The force field depleted the Sword's ability to protect itself so it transferred its power elsewhere to guard against Clygon harnessing its power for evil."

"Where did the power… Wait a minute. You think it transferred its power to the sword on my wall? That's why Blythar came? *RiverHome* is dying and unprotected. You needed my sword!"

"Clever as always, Toby Baxter." Clovor smiled at him.

"But how? Why? When you were explaining the Sword to me the last time I was here, I asked if the Sword was magic. You said that it's complicated, but yes, it's magic. What did you mean?"

Clovor closed her eyes and began to hum. Toby had come to learn that for the river elves, singing the story is a better way of telling it.

"Long ago the giants and the river elves entered into an Alliance of Friendship. Our two peoples committed to working for peace not only between us but throughout the land. We also agreed to trade goods and share new knowledge and wisdom.

"The giants were forgers of metal, imbuing their work with ancient magic."

"What does imbuing mean?"

"It means to permeate. The giants permeated their creations with magic—magic that was always and only used for good—to preserve peace.

"To seal the Alliance, the giants presented the river elves with two identical Swords. One of the Swords was forged with magic. The other was created as a back-up sword of sorts, with a hint of magic, in case the magic of the first Sword was ever in jeopardy.

"The first Sword has served as our protector ever since, calling the HERO to us in times of threat. The second sword found its way to your world where it has been passed from one generation of Baxters to the next."

"That's the sword my Grandma Baxter gave to me for my birthday."

"Yes, the sword *Loach*." She'd stopped singing and was talking again.

"So that explains why my dad and me…"

"My dad and I…" Clovor corrected.

"I'm on Winter Break. No grammar until I'm back in school!"

"Break or no break, Toby, it's important to keep your mind sharp—and working on your grammar is a good way to do that."

Blah… blah… bl…

"What's that?" Clovor asked.

He fake-coughed.

"Ah… um… that explains why my dad and I can feel a current of energy when we hold *Loach*. To think it's been hanging on my wall for the last few months! And that explains why, when I planted it in the stone back at *RiverHome*…"

"It began to bring life back to the land," Clovor finished his sentence. "And *Loach* has brought you back to *RiverHome*, as well."

Toby took a moment to ponder. *Ponder? Really?*

"What do you think Clygon is doing with the Sword?"

"I'm guessing he has his tech team working on it, trying to figure out how to jumpstart the magic, in the hope of using it himself."

"Tech team?"

"Tech isn't just an iPhone, or iPad, or computer game, Toby. Tech is any tool that helps us in life. Like a pencil. Or a fork. Or a sleigh. Or a magic sword. Or toilet paper."

Oreeo interrupted them.

"We're almost there."

Toby then asked Clovor the question that had been bothering him.

"I… um… ah… I didn't see Grandpa back at Command Central."

Before Clovor could respond, two small objects hit them on the head. Toby picked them up. *Nose plugs?*

"Put them on," demanded Oreeo. He had two on his big schnoz.

"Why?" Toby asked.

"Put. Them. On."

As they put on their nose plugs, Toby looked over the side of the sleigh and saw up ahead, glowing in the thick falling snow, the lights of what must be *Ogreton Heights*. It looked strangely magical. But it felt foreboding.

With Oreeo, once again, facing the front of the sleigh, Toby quickly removed his nose plug. And instantly he knew why they were being forced to wear them. He nudged Clovor to do the same and she, too, understood.

They smelled hope.

9

Angel from the Realm of Glory

Sid's brain circuits were on overload. While still trying to get his bearings in this new wherever-he-was, he caught little bits and pieces of the conversations going on around him.

"…we were just coming to the entrance when we saw Clovor and Toby, both sound asleep, being carried to a sleigh by ogres…"

"…I led Toby to *RiverHome*, Thomas. He put *Loach* in the stone and then we headed here…"

"…but that means Toby doesn't have the sword with him… he's not safe…"

"…Thomas, remember, the Sword, or in this case, *Loach*, always finds the HERO…"

"…this is my cousin, Mathilda…" This said directly to Sid by Deckor.

But what brought him back into the present was the sound of multiple weapons being unsheathed and a woman crying out, "Wait!"

He turned toward the voice and saw two women, swords and daggers pointed at them by the river elves.

The first woman was a river elf soldier, judging by her armor. Like the other elves she was about five-feet-tall, had Mr Spock eyebrows, with the pointy tips of her ears poking out from behind her short, brown hair. Her armor covered most of her body and it bore the scratches of a battle. Blood seeped out of a big gash across her right cheek and she had to lean on the second woman to stay standing.

It was the second woman who held Sid's attention. She was a goddess. Otherworldly. She stood about his size and was also dressed in battle gear. She had long, deep red hair flowing out from under her helmet, skin as dark as his, and big, round, beautiful sea-blue eyes. Sid was sure he saw small stars float out of her eyes when she blinked. She held a shield and sword in her free hand, the other hand and arm holding up the river elf soldier. She reminded him a bit of a female Thor. The lingering but quickly melting snow on her shoulders made her glow. A snow angel! He couldn't take his eyes off of her. He was in the full throes of an oxytocin rush.

"Johanna, explain yourself," Donold demanded.

"Put your swords down, Donold. She's not a threat."

Sid watched out of the corner of his eye as a male elf made his way to the one called Johanna and began to quietly hum over her while checking out her wounds.

"Look around you, Johanna. Her people drugged us and kidnapped Clovor and Toby Baxter." Donold held up a half-eaten Eogre Egg while nodding toward the river elves still trying to wake up.

So, she's an ogre, Sid thought, his mouth hanging open as he continued to stare at her.

"She's not our enemy, Donold. Trust me. Let us sit down. Give us something to drink. And I'll explain everything."

Sid sensed the swords and daggers being sheathed. He watched as Johanna was led by the humming elf and the snow angel to a chair. Goblets were brought to them and both women took a long drink of whatever was in them.

The humming elf continued whatever he was doing to Johanna's injuries and Mathilda pulled up a chair next to her, sat down, and put her arm around Johanna's shoulder.

"Take your time, Johanna," Mathilda said quietly.

"WE DON'T HAVE TIME," Donold shouted. But Mathilda's withering look silenced him.

"It's okay," Johanna said. "Donold's right. You need to hear our story."

The ogre goddess suddenly looked over at Sid and caught him staring at her. She winked at him and Sid was sure he turned red, then orange, and then red again. He was gobsmacked. *Gobsmacked? Is that even a word?*

***

Phoenix saw the rainbow of colors on Sid's face and nudged Thomas with his shoulder.

"Look at our friend, Sid. He's been hit."

Thomas chuckled and whispered to Phoenix, "And hard! Looks like he has a bad case of puppy love."

As he said puppy love, Phoenix at the same time said, "Dragon love."

"Puppy love?" laughed Phoenix.

"Dragon love?" asked Thomas.

Thomas, smiling at Sid's goofy puppy/dragon love smile, said, "It hit me the moment I laid eyes on Jan in high school. It was love at first sight."

"Is Jan your wife?"

Thomas nodded. "How about you? Have you been hit with dragon love, as you call it?"

"Yup," Phoenix replied. "The first time I saw Roxie in the last book…"

"Last book?" Thomas asked. "What are you talking about?"

Phoenix hemmed and hawed.

"I meant the last time Toby was here."

Thomas stared at him until Phoenix looked away.

"Is Author writing books about Toby?"

Phoenix didn't answer.

"Well, is he?"

Phoenix was saved by Sid who let out a sigh so loud that everyone turned to see what was wrong.

Thomas and Phoenix laughed out loud until Mathilda aimed her withering look at them.

***

Johanna began her story.

"We were out on patrol near the *River Glaedaan,* about ten miles south of here. We saw nothing. No tracks. We heard nothing. At least nothing to cause alarm. Then out of nowhere, about fifty trolls ambushed us. I can't for the life of me figure out how they flat-footed us. We put up a good fight but were caught off-guard. Most of us sustained injuries… we lost five…" Johanna's voice caught.

"They rounded up the rest of us and started leading us deeper south, sticking close to the river. After about three miles, they stopped and tied everyone up. We waited for an hour when Plythar arrived."

Sid, his eyes still firmly on the snow angel, felt the eyes of all the others turn to look at someone.

"What did he want?" Blythar asked. "What did he do?"

"He consulted with one of his soldiers then nodded at us. I knew then that we were in trouble."

"Why?" asked Mathilda.

"Because he recognized Judah."

Somewhere earlier in the bits of conversation Sid had learned that Judah was Mathilda's brother.

"Judah!" Mathilda said with some alarm. "What was he doing with you? I thought he was in the north?"

"He had been. But he was convinced that all of the action was in the south. He and his scouts caught up with us a few weeks ago. When the trolls captured us, we tried to hide him in the middle of our group. But Plythar spotted him immediately. He had Judah brought to him, tied his hands behind his back, and then headed off south."

"It's that curly blonde hair!" Phoenix said, trying to lighten the mood.

Mathilda stood up and paced the room. She turned to Blythar.

"What game is your brother playing?"

Blythar, surprised by her anger, flinched and backed away a step or two.

"I... I'm... I don't know. It makes no sense. He let me and Toby go. He let Phoenix, Deckor, Thomas, and Sid go. He gave us Esther Eggs. Maybe he needs Judah's help? Maybe he needed to look like he's still on Clygon's side?" Blythar shook his head, his eyes pleading with them to believe in his brother.

Mathilda walked up to him and put a hand on his arm.

"Sorry, Blythar. Sorry. The news shocked me. I trust you. You know that. And if you trust your brother, I trust him too."

Turning to Johanna, Mathilda said, "Go on."

"From then on, most of it is a blur," Johanna continued. "We heard a loud scream and our ogre friend here, and some of her troops, ran off the trolls. After attending to the wounded, the two of us made haste to get here as soon as we could."

The room fell silent, except for Sid's beating heart.

"And you are?" Donold turned on the ogre.

Sid wanted to punch him.

"Manners, Donold!" An elderly woman, leaning on Deckor, came from out of nowhere and walked up to the snow angel.

"Don't mind him," she said. "He's having a very bad day."

The ogre woman smiled. *Were those little hearts dancing around the corners of her smile?*

55

"My name is Oreea." She pronounced it OrEEah.

To Sid's ears, she had the voice of a lioness—deep, rich, mesmerizing. And she had a name. Oreea! OrEEah. Sid's heart moved into another gear.

"Oreea?" Thomas said. "Do you have a brother by the name of Oreeo? Like the cookie?"

"I do," she said with her beautiful, light-up-the-room smile. "How do you know him?"

"When I was here during the Troll War, I was surrounded during one of the battles and about to have a sword rammed into my shoulder. But in the nick of time, a young ogre came out of nowhere, fought through the circle of troll soldiers, grabbed me and carried me back to Phoenix and Deckor."

"I remember that," Deckor said. "He tipped his sword to us, said, 'My name is Oreeo,' and then he disappeared. I'd completely forgotten about that."

At that moment Sid saw the room darken and the rain clouds come in as Oreea's beautiful smile turned to a frown.

"Oreeo is now captain of our army. He's sold himself to the trolls. He's become a mercenary and has convinced most of our army to join him."

"He was here." It was Roxie. "I'm sure of it. He was the one who took Clovor and Toby."

The room fell silent once again.

"May I suggest," the elderly woman said, "that we let the Healer finish up with Johanna and we serve our guest something to eat. I'm guessing there is a lot to talk about."

As the elves began to move about, Mathilda introduced herself to Oreea.

"These are my cousins, Phoenix and Deckor. And this is Thomas Baxter."

Oreea shook their hands and said to Thomas, "I know of your son!"

"And this," Mathilda said, "is Sid, a friend of Toby's and Thomas's."

Oreea walked over to Sid, placed her hand on his shoulder, and said, "It is so nice to meet you, young Sid."

Sid felt his knees buckle. *She said my name!* Thankfully, Phoenix was there to hold him up. Sid opened his mouth to return her greeting but nothing came out.

"I think Sid is in love," Deckor whispered to Mathilda.

Donold began issuing orders.

"Victor. Ethol. Take twelve elves and stand guard outside. Roxie, can you and your gnomes use your remarkable packing skills to help us pack up what we need? We need to move as soon as possible. We've been compromised. Oreea, Deckor, Mathilda, Thomas, Blythar, and Johanna, join me at the Command Table. We need to regroup. And Phoenix, perhaps you can help our new friend, Sid, come back down to earth."

Donold let out a huge laugh and headed to the table.

As everyone started carrying out Donold's orders, a poem took shape in Sid's mind:

Oreea. Oreea.
The stars shine above-ee-a.
Oreea. Oreea.
I think I'm in love-ee-a.

Reviewing the poem in his mind so that he wouldn't forget it, Sid thought, *I'm a pretty good poet!*

"Wow," Phoenix said, taking Sid by the arm. "That was really lame."

Sid froze. Had Phoenix heard his homage to Oreea? *Homage? Love has really opened him up to big words… Had he said the poem out loud?* But he quickly realized that Phoenix was making fun of him for not being able to speak to her.

"She's old enough to be your mom!" Phoenix laughed.

"I have no idea what or whom you are talking about," Sid answered defensively.

"Is it who? Or whom?" Phoenix asked. "And yes, you do! Oreea. Oreea. I think I'm in love-ee-a."

Sid turned red, then orange, then red once again, again.

"Don't worry, Sid. It's our secret. It happens to the best of us. For me, it was my second-grade teacher, Miss Midge. The sun rose and set with each and every one of her smiles."

Phoenix patted Sid on the back.

"Come on. Let's grab a bite of food."

Sid, not watching where he was going, accidently bumped into Oreea. She didn't notice, thankfully. But the electricity up and down his spine lasted for what seemed like several minutes.

He was brought back to reality when a big wolf jumped up, put her paws on his shoulders, and gave him a big, sloppy kiss.

"I see you've met Saanti," Phoenix said with a grin.

10

Little Drummer Boy

Plythar walked behind Judah, prodding him from time to time with his sword to keep him moving. And from time to time, Judah would turn back to Plythar with a look that would make a normal person wither with fear. Plythar, however, was no normal person. He met the look with a smirk.

Judah's arms, tied behind his back, had grown numb. Walking in the increasingly thick snow didn't make things easier. He was frustrated with himself for being ambushed. And he was anxious about what might have happened to Johanna and the *RiverHome* scouts.

Plythar slowed and then stopped. He stood quietly as if listening for something. Judah found himself likewise on high alert. A snapping of a tree branch to his left confirmed the sense he had had for a while. They were being watched.

From out of the trees stepped a young male troll. He was squat. Tufts of unkempt hair sprouted in various directions out of his head with the usual straw hair coming out of his ears. His stinky troll smell caused Judah's eyes to water.

Judah turned to look at Plythar and saw Plythar smile. At the same time, Plythar cut the ropes that held Judah's hands. Judah shook his arms to get the feeling back, now curious about what was happening.

Plythar stepped away from Judah and quietly talked with the young troll. After several minutes, Plythar and the young troll made their way to Judah.

"Judah of *RiverHome*," Plythar said, "this is Drummer. Drummer, this is Judah, obviously a river elf."

Drummer bowed to Judah, then reached out to shake his hand. Judah was so shocked by this show of hospitality from an enemy that he didn't move for a moment. Then he slowly offered his hand to Drummer. Drummer's hand felt like course sandpaper.

"He doesn't know what's up yet, does he, Plythar?" Drummer said, nodding at Judah.

Plythar nodded but said nothing.

"What's he talking about?" asked Judah. "What's going on?"

"Not here," Plythar said. "Too many eyes…"

An arrow hit Plythar just above his knee, sending him to the ground.

"Run!" he shouted.

Without hesitation, Drummer grabbed Judah and headed down a path Judah couldn't see through the snow and the trees. Behind them, they heard voices. *Ogre voices?*

"What's going on?" Judah yelled while gasping for breath.

"Not now. Keep… running," Drummer shouted.

They ran—trudged was more like it—as fast as they could in and out of trees. They turned left. Then right. Up a hill. Then down a hill. The snow was now so thick that Judah could barely see his feet, let alone a path. He knew that if he didn't stick close to Drummer he'd be lost.

After about fifteen minutes, Drummer stopped and leaned up against a tree. Judah did the same. They spent several minutes trying to catch their breath, hyper-sensitive to the sounds around them. Unfortunately, the thick snow acted as a muffle.

Judah noticed that, as Drummer gulped in air, he was tapping his fingers on his knees while his head nodded along to whatever rhythm he was hearing in his mind.

"Is that… why… they call you… Drummer?" Judah said between deep breaths, nodding to the tapping hands.

Drummer looked up at him. "I… I… just a minute."

Drummer took a big deep breath and slowly let it out.

"That helps. My name is Klythar. In my spare time, I play drums for a nineties troll tribute band. I always have a song in my head. Hence the nickname, Drummer."

"A nineties troll tribute band?"

"Yah. You know. Music from bands like Nirvana. Or Sound Garden. Some Green Day. We even throw in some U2 for the old folks."

"Where did you hear about that kind of…?"

"Sorry. No time to chat. We have a few miles to go." He handed Judah a piece of jerky. After eating it, Judah melted some snow in his mouth for hydration.

"Where? Where are we headed?"

But Drummer was already jog-trudging through the snow.

Thirty minutes later Drummer stopped. He waited. Judah was about to ask him again what was going on when a gnome and an ogre appeared, seemingly out of nowhere. Drummer nodded to them and then to Judah, indicating that he and Judah were to follow the two strangers.

Now almost completely dark, the gnome and ogre lit torches to help guide the way. Within a minute, they stood before a mound, surrounded by trees. A door opened and Judah followed Drummer, the gnome, and the ogre through it into a beehive of activity.

He saw trolls, gnomes, and ogres huddled in groups, pouring over maps, preparing weapons, or eating. Some slept on makeshift cots.

"Ho! Friend Judah!"

Judah turned toward the voice and was shocked to see Jerry, a gnome and also Roxie's dad. Next to Jerry was his faithful wolf, Saaba, whose injury from their last battle with Clygon appeared completely healed.

"Jerry!" He high-fived his friend, although Jerry, much shorter than Judah, had to jump up a bit to hit Judah's hand. "Where are we? What are you doing here? What is this?"

"This, Friend Judah, is the center of the Resistance."

11

Blue Christmas

"I met your dad once, back during the Troll and Elf War," Oreeo said over his shoulder as he led Toby and Clovor into *Ogreton Heights*. "He was surrounded by trolls and about to take a sword to his shoulder. I swept in and saved him. He owes me." His voice sounded nasally with the nose plug on.

Toby winced at the thought of his dad being sliced up by a troll.

"So, if you were at least friendly to the river elf cause once upon a time, why are you now siding with our enemy?" Clovor asked.

The snow crunched under their feet as they moved toward the door of a massive tower.

"Money, of course," Oreeo said. "And power, of course. Clygon has promised me the position of his commander when we finally break the power of the Sword and the heroes."

"Not gonna happen," Toby muttered under his breath, which was hard to do with a nose plug on.

"What was that, hero?"

"I said, it sounds promising."

"Good answer. And prophetic too. As you'll see in no time."

Oreeo led them into a tower. It took a moment for their eyes to adjust to the torches, the haze, and the twelve swords all pointed at them.

"Now, now, now, men, is that any way to treat our honored guests?" Oreeo motioned for the guards to lower their weapons. "We have with us today the esteemed commander of the river elves, Clovor of *RiverHome,* and the legendary hero, Toby Baxter."

Off in the distance, Toby heard what sounded like an animal being tortured. He shuddered.

"Music to my ears," Oreeo said, nodding toward the sound. "Not to worry, hero Toby. Clygon has something much different in mind for you and your friends. Follow me."

Oreeo waved off the guards and led Toby and Clovor deeper into the Keep, as Oreeo called it. It was a dismal place. The cold walls were made of stone. It was pitch dark in the corners where the torch light didn't reach. Prison cells lined part of the way, seemingly empty.

"They'll be full soon enough," Oreeo said, as if reading Toby's mind.

Clovor grabbed Toby's hand to reassure him.

Eventually, they found themselves in a large banquet hall. The room was brightly lit with a warm fire off to the side. The huge table was loaded with food—from the looks of it, the kind of food that Toby's family ate at Christmas: turkey, mashed potatoes, ham, green bean casserole, apple pie. His mouth watered to the point of drooling.

Oreeo pointed to a couple of chairs with their backs facing the fireplace.

"Have a seat. I'm guessing you're hungry and might want to enjoy one final feast." Oreeo thought that was extremely funny but the humor was lost on Toby.

As they were seated, three trolls emerged from an unseen doorway. When Toby saw them, he gasped. #41! #42! #43! They had been servant trolls under Clygon when Toby was last in *RiverHome*, only to be liberated when Toby used the Sword to create the force field. They had taken on names to celebrate their freedom from Clygon's tyranny: Prothar, Sythar, and Thytar. Toby noticed they were shuffling and saw chains around their ankles. He could feel their humiliation.

They nodded at him and Clovor, poured each of them something to drink, and put food on their plates. Then they were gone.

Toby felt the anger taking over again. He looked down at his hands and saw a faint glow. He wasn't quite sure how this was possible without the Sword but maybe Clovor was right when she told him on his last visit that the Sword was an extension of his power.

He suddenly felt Clovor's elbow in his arm. "Breathe, Toby. Breathe," she whispered.

"Bon appetite," Oreeo said as he hoisted a mug and took a swig.

"It's bon appetit, you lunk..."

"Breathe, Toby. Breathe!"

"Not so easy with this nose plug thingy!"

Oblivious to what was happening across the table from him, Oreeo said, "I profusely apologize that our Prime Minister cannot be with you to welcome you this evening. I'm sorry to say..." at this Oreeo snickered, "...he's been circumscribed."

"Circum-what?" Toby grimaced in horror.

"He doesn't mean that, Toby. He means the Prime Minister has been detained, imprisoned, incarcerated... choose your own synonym."

"Syno-what?" Oreeo asked.

A large noise, sounding like some kind of skirmish down the hallway, broke into their meal. At first, it was shouting. Then the sound of sword against sword. A guard rushed in and whispered something to Oreeo. Oreeo did not look pleased. He threw his napkin down onto the table, stood up, pushing his chair back so hard it slid into the wall, and said to the guard, "Get my sword."

"You two," he said to Toby and Clovor, all jauntiness—*jauntiness?*— gone from his demeanor—*demeanor? Slow it down, Author!* "stay here. Enjoy the food. You can run if you'd like but there is nowhere to go."

And with that, Oreeo left the hall.

At that same moment, Prothar, Sythar, and Thytar returned to pour more drinks.

"Is there a way out of here?" Clovor asked. "One perhaps the ogres don't know about or have forgotten?"

Sythar nodded, yes.

"If we didn't have these chains on we'd take you. It's too hard to explain," Prothar said in despair.

A primal scream filled the hall. It was Toby. The stress of the moment, the lack of sleep, and his irritation at his own lack of any superhero powers exploded out of him.

Clovor, Prothar, Sythar, and Thytar stared at him.

Then Clovor began to laugh. She laughed so hard that tears ran down her cheeks.

"Do you... feel... better?" she asked, holding her side.

"What's so funny?" Toby asked, embarrassed and miffed, whatever miffed meant.

Toby stared at Clovor as she continued to laugh. But he noticed that the tears didn't seem to be tears of laughter.

"Wait a minute," he said. "Your laughter... it's the same as my scream! You're scared, too! You're frustrated, too!"

"Toby Baxter, you never cease to amaze me! But enough talk about how we vent our fears. We need to act."

"Come with us," Thytar said as he shuffled as quickly as possible to the kitchen door. "We'll do our best to point you in the right direction."

Just as they were about to go through the kitchen door Sythar groaned. Before Toby could see the source of her dismay, something hit him. Hard. On the head…

***

It was the snoring that woke him up. Long, deep snoring. Loud snoring. Contented snoring if snoring can sound contented.

He sat up on one arm. His head hurt. He rubbed the tender knot left by whatever had hit him. He looked around. The room was lit with a soft blue haze. Off to his left, he saw whom he assumed was Clovor. To his right. he noticed huge boots, attached to huge long legs, attached to the Christmas Giant, his back against the wall. Sound asleep.

Toby quickly pulled his nose plug off hoping for an energizing whiff of hope. But it wasn't there. He couldn't smell it. What he smelled instead was… was… *sadness? Despair? Depression?* It threatened to overwhelm him.

He sat up. Then he stood up. He was now face level with the sleeping giant.

The giant snorted. Rubbed his nose. Dropped his oversized arm back to his side. Then he sneezed, knocking Toby backwards, covering him with giant spit.

Gross!

Toby wiped off his face, walked up again to the giant, and shook his massive shoulder.

The giant stirred. He opened an eye and looked at Toby. He smiled at Toby. A big, huge, happy smile. Then promptly fell back to sleep, as the blue enveloped Toby with hopelessness.

12

All I Want for Christmas is You

Sid stood off in the corner still trying to take in all that was happening. Ogres! Trolls! Elves! Gnomes! Wolves! Oreea! His head was spinning.

"May I sit with you?" The elderly, frail-looking woman sat down next to him.

She was the smallest elf he had ever seen, although admittedly he'd only seen a handful of elves. She was almost half his size. Her long, gray, braided hair reached down to her mid-back, accentuating her pointy ears. Her skin was grayish as were her Mr Spock eyebrows, her face lined with the long years she had lived. On her small nose sat reading glasses. *Can reading glasses sit?* She wore a jacket over a dark tunic and pants, along with the big, hairy boots.

She put her small, wrinkled hand on his.

"I'm Grandma."

Sid looked at her for a moment. He thought he could see a resemblance.

"Phoenix? Deckor? Mathilda?"

"Yes, and Judah and Clovor too. Grandpa and I..."

She choked back a sob.

"Sorry, we recently lost Grandpa. We'd been married for such a long time..."

Sid squeezed her hand.

"Grandpa and I raised our five grandchildren after their parents died in the Troll War some twenty-six or so of your years ago. I have a hard time keeping track of time right now. That was when we first met Thomas."

Even though she was elderly and grieving, Sid could see the brightness in her eyes.

"You must be discombobulated. Thomas and Toby had the same experience. Now they're part of the family, and so are you, Sid."

He looked over at the Command Table, wondering what they were talking about. He watched the gnomes scurrying about putting essentials into backpacks, including shovels and hand wipes. He felt out of place and useless.

"Don't worry, Sid. You'll find your place here soon enough…"

"Dagnabit!" The curse came hurling down the stairway, along with a cold burst of air. Everyone grabbed their weapons and pointed them toward the sound.

"Watch what you're doing, you lunk-headed ogre. Get out of my way! I can do this mys…"

And with that, a troll came tumbling down the stairs, landing on his back.

"Plythar!" Blythar shouted as he ran to his brother. "What are you doing here?" Blythar helped his brother to his feet but Plythar had to lean on him.

"What am I doing here? Ask those blankety-blank ogres what I'm doing here! Ask them why they shot me in the leg with an arrow! Ask them why they're taking up oxygen!"

Noticing a bloody rag around Plythar's knee, the Healer—Sid had just been introduced to him moments earlier—moved over to Plythar, helped Blythar get him into a chair, and began to work on the wound.

Four sheepish-looking ogre soldiers peered out from the stairs. Oreea saw them.

"Explain," she said.

Sid watched as one of the ogres, a male, who had the body of a god, the long flowing hair of a romance book cover character, but small, too-close-together eyes and a big—make that huge—nose, stepped forward and saluted Oreea.

"My Lady," he said. "After you drove off the trolls, we noticed two sets of tracks leading south. We followed them and found this troll with one of the river elves…"

"It must have been Judah," Mathilda said.

"We thought the river elf was a captive of the troll so we…"

"So you shot me in the knee!"

"If they had wanted to do you harm, troll… let's just say, they never miss their target," Oreea said with humor.

"The river elf ran off with what looked like a troll. This one here," he nodded to Plythar, "told us to bring him here, which we found strange, to say the least. But once we were convinced that he is with the Resistance, we felt it important to get him here as soon as possible."

"Have you been compromised?" asked Blythar.

"No, I don't think so," Plythar said, calming down under the influence of the Healer.

"Tell us what you know," Donold said. "We're leaving in twenty minutes. Unlike you, we have been compromised."

Blythar helped his brother to his feet and held him as they stood at the Command Table. When they learned of a Resistance cave down south, toward *Ogreton Heights*, they decided to head there. Plythar said that's where Judah would be.

Mathilda walked over to Sid and Grandma.

"Here," she said. "Put these on."

She handed him a pair of big, hairy-looking boots along with a light-weight hooded overcoat. All white, presumably to blend in with the snow, although his dark face would surely stand out.

"And take this." She handed him a huge, full-as-can-be backpack. He was sure it weighed at least sixty pounds but found it light and easy to carry.

Donold called everyone together.

"Our scouts will go out in two groups to ensure the safest passage to the Resistance. The gnomes will disperse and recruit more help and meet us there. Oreea and her soldiers will accompany us. Their intel will prove invaluable once we get near *Ogreton Heights*.

"Plythar. What will you do?"

"I'm still on the inside with Clygon. Best I find my way back to him and learn what I can."

Donold nodded.

With that, everyone formed a circle. They joined hands and began to hum. Celtic music. Sid could feel it in his bones. Soothing. Encouraging. Energizing. He'd maybe need to download some Enya songs when he got back home. *If he got back home…*

"Creator," Sid looked up to see Grandma standing in the middle of the circle, her hands in the air as if blessing the group. Her voice strong. Her eyes alive.

"I pray for my friends. I pray for their safety. Grant them wisdom. Grant them courage. Grant them hope. Grant them compassion…"

Sid heard Plythar grunt.

"…and use them to bring peace back to the land."

With that, the humming stopped.

"Donold," Grandma said. "I'd like to request that Ethol accompany me home. My place is there. Perhaps I can bring some aid to any of our river elf friends in hiding."

Donold nodded. Mathilda hugged her. So did Deckor and Phoenix. As did Thomas. Sid didn't know what to do but Grandma did and hugged him. She was remarkably strong for such an elderly, small woman.

They climbed the stairs and found themselves in the middle of a snow storm. The snow was so thick that it was hard to see. The wind didn't help. Nor the darkness.

"Stay close to me, Sid," Phoenix said.

"What about Thomas?" Sid asked.

"I'm here, Sid. Deckor has my back."

Several of the river elves held what had to be magical torches, as the snow and the wind didn't seem to have the power to extinguish them. He could see Blythar and Plythar shake hands and watched as Plythar headed off to wherever he was headed. He saw the gnomes, along with Roxie and her wolf, Saanti, break off to go wherever they were going.

Then they were moving. Slowly. Into the storm. For what seemed like hours. Silently.

Finally, they stopped for a short rest.

Sid dug into his backpack and grabbed what looked like an energy bar. He took a big bite of it. It was quite tasty.

"How do you like this adventure so far?" Thomas whispered.

Sid smiled for the first time in who knows how long.

"If I weren't so confused and terrified I might actually…"

HO! HO! HO!

Everyone froze.

From behind the trees, the smell of vomit hit them, along with light from torches. They were surrounded.

A big, round, heavily-coated-in-animal-skin troll moved from out of the group.

Deckor groaned.

"Clygon!" Donold said, his sword drawn.

"Donny, how nice to see you again," he snarled, "and all of your pathetic friends. You might as well drop your weapons. You're surrounded, as you can see."

Sid felt Phoenix grab his right arm. He felt Mathilda grab his left. They slowly backed up, trusting the snow and their white clothes to camouflage them.

"Thomas Baxter," Clygon said. "I was just telling my friend, Plythar, here, that all I wanted for Christmas was you! And Toby, of course. And here you are."

Plythar stepped out of the shadows.

"Plythar," Clygon said. "Why don't you grab our friend, Thomas. And for good measure, let's bring Donny with us as well. Oh... and is that the Healer? The more the merrier. And of course, let's take Dickle too..."

"It's Deckor," Deckor growled.

"And is that Oreeo's sister I see? He'll be so very happy to have you back home. The rest of you, don't move or follow us. You won't like the consequences."

Clygon laughed. A hideous, screeching laugh.

By this point, Phoenix, Mathilda, and Sid were far enough away that they were able to quietly run back toward *RiverHome*.

The last words they heard were, "Where's Toby's friend? Not here? No worries. Once he knows what we have planned for you and Toby, he and his little elf friends will find us!"

13

Santa Claus is Coming to Town

He heard whispers coming to him from out of his sleepy haze. One of the voices belonged to Clovor. He looked around, remembering now that he had been hit on the head and was in a cell, somewhere in *Ogreton Heights*. If this keeps up he'll likely end up concussed on one of these visits to *RiverHome!*

The blues had subsided and he began to feel a bit of hope again.

"Ah, Toby! Good morning! Nice to see your bright, shiny face on this fine day." It was the giant, but the voice, as always, was that of his Grandpa Baxter.

"Our friend, Clovor, was telling me a bit about your adventure so far. I'm honored to hear that you set out to rescue me. Looks like you found me. Or, maybe better said, it looks like I found you!" The giant winked at Clovor and laughed a big, hearty Ho! Ho! Ho! Santa-worthy laugh.

Toby massaged the bump on his head.

"I don't know what that means," he said.

He looked over at Clovor. She was a ball of excitement. Of course! She was meeting the Christmas Giant for the first time. She seemed so very small next to him. But she didn't seem intimidated.

"He sounds like my grandpa," she whispered to Toby.

"Interesting! He sounds like my grandpa to me," he whispered back.

The door to the cell opened. An ogre guard, wearing a nose plug, quickly put a tray of food down, backed out of the cell, and locked it.

Toby realized he was hungry. His stomach growled. At the same time, he felt a bit woozy.

He meandered over to the food—*meandered?*—and was surprised to find that it looked and smelled pretty good. Three pieces of bread—an extra-large one, presumably for the giant—and cheese slices, along with a water jug and three cups.

He carried the tray over to Clovor and the giant. They quickly downed the small feast.

After a big gulp of water, Toby said, "Why was it blue in here yesterday? Why couldn't I smell hope?"

"They drugged you, Toby. And you too, Clovor."

"Drugged us? Why?"

"They've had a bit of a challenge since I've been here," the giant laughed. "Hope keeps seeping into their souls. And when they smell hope, they want to tear down the ugliness in this place and replace it with goodness. All kinds of skirmishes break out here every day when someone takes off a nose plug or the drug wears off. It was that kind of fracas that ultimately led you here."

"Fracas?" Toby asked.

"Same as skirmish," Clovor said.

The giant let out a big, contented sigh. "I have to admit, I've really been enjoying myself."

Toby took another drink of water and shook his head, trying to get the remaining cobwebs out. *How do you get cobwebs in your head?*

He looked over at Clovor.

"Can I ask you something?"

Clovor nodded.

"What happened to your grandpa?"

Her face clouded over. The giant too, seemed saddened by the question.

"We're not really sure," she said, choking back tears. "When the Sword began to lose its power, Grandpa began to weaken. It seemed as if his life was tied to the life of the Sword. We lost him within a few months of the force field failing. Thankfully, we were with him at the end and he... died peacefully."

She let out a big sigh. As did the giant.

Toby sometimes felt embarrassed in the face of the emotions of someone else. He wasn't sure why. And he never knew exactly what to do.

"I'm... so sorry, Clovor." He hesitantly put his hand on her arm. She placed her hand on his and squeezed it.

The giant leaned forward and put his big arms around the two of them.

After several moments, Toby asked the giant, "So, what's the plan?"

The giant leaned back against the wall.

"I'm not sure what you mean, Toby," the giant said. "What plan?"

"Why are you here? Why are we here? And how do we get out of here and find the Sword?"

The giant laughed. Another big, hearty, Santa laugh. A laugh almost too big for a giant stuck in a cell.

"That would be cheating, Toby. What fun would it be if we knew the ending before we got there?"

"O... kay...," Toby said. "So, how about this? Why are you here? You're the Christmas Giant. How in *RiverHome* did you end up in prison?"

"I turned myself in, of course."

"Of course you did," muttered Toby. "And why, of course, did you do that?"

"Two reasons. First, to get you back here, Toby."

Toby was momentarily stunned.

"Why would you want to get me back here?"

"Because I think we both know you have some unfinished business."

"Huh?"

"Remember how you felt after planting the Sword in the ground?"

Toby looked down sheepishly. "I... uh... um... was a bit... um... embarrassed."

"Why was that?

"Because it didn't seem to be very heroic. I didn't slay any Voldemorts. I didn't outmaneuver any Gollums. I didn't stand up to any Greek or Roman gods. I didn't face down any Daleks. I didn't go toe to toe with Thanos. I just..."

"You just what, Toby?" Clovor jumped in.

"I just planted the Sword in the ground. And look at what happened. The Sword is back in Clygon's hands, he's on the move again and the giant is in prison and so are we. Not very heroic."

"But look at what happened to you, Toby," Clovor said. "As you held that Sword you had a decision to make: would you use your power to match violence with violence or would you choose a better path? You drew a line in the sand. At that moment, you chose the better way. You chose the kind of man you are going to be. That line in the sand was more about you than it was about Clygon. And that decision, for a while anyway, brought peace to *RiverHome*, and made many enemies into friends. You made that happen."

Blah. Blah. Blah.

"Did you just blah blah blah me again?" Both Clovor and the giant laughed.

Toby instinctively looked up to see if the words had been printed above his head. Nothing. *How does she do that?*

"That's why you're here, Toby," the giant said in Grandpa Baxter's voice. "You're just getting started. There's more to your HERO's journey ahead."

"About that," Toby said. "It doesn't feel like much of a quest."

"Explain," Clovor said.

"Well, we don't seem to be going anywhere or doing anything. We've been prisoners for most of my time here so far."

"Ah, young Toby," the giant said. "A quest isn't just about going somewhere or doing something. It's also about becoming."

"Becoming what?"

"A HERO, of course."

The giant reached his hand into one of his pockets and pulled out a small box.

"Here. This is for you, Toby."

Toby opened it. It was a compass.

"Is this the same compass I used last time?" Toby asked.

"Look more closely."

Toby noticed the coordinates were different. Instead of H-E-R-O, this compass read: W-I-S-E.

"WISE?"

"Yes, Toby, Part of the quest to become a HERO is to become WISE. Wisdom is an essential part of being a HERO. And soon, it will be the gift that will save *RiverHome.*"

Clovor moved over to look at the compass. "What do the letters stand for?" she asked.

"The W stands for Wonder: Be Curious!"

"What has that got to do with being a hero?" Toby asked.

The giant stroked his beard.

"Have you ever wondered why Clygon is Clygon? Why he has so much anger in his life?"

"No. I just assumed he is mean, maniacal, hard-hearted, nasty..."

"Okay, Toby," Clovor put her hand on his arm. "We get it."

"Is he though?" the giant asked. As he did, he looked off into space, as if remembering something.

More to himself than to Toby and Clovor, the giant said, "He reminds me of Scrooge."

73

"Scrooge?" Toby asked, incredulously—*or is it incredulous? Wait—no grammar! I'm on a break!*—rubbing the bump on the back of his noggin. "My mom asked me to read a book along with her this Christmas about Scrooge. I didn't get past the first paragraph. He's the guy who's visited by three wise men…"

He shook his head.

"Wait. That doesn't sound right."

"Ghosts, Toby, three ghosts. The wise men are in a different Christmas story," Clovor said.

"Oops," Toby laughed. "I know that. My pastor would be a bit disappointed with me," he smiled, "but, in all fairness, that knock on the head knocked some stuff out of my head, I think. Ghosts. Got it. But Scrooge isn't real, right? He's just a story."

"Is he, Toby? Are you just a story?"

That was far too existential for Toby, whatever existential meant.

"Many described Scrooge as you just described Clygon—mean, nasty, hard-hearted. That's how he was when I visited him…"

"Wait! What? You visited Scrooge?"

"Of course. I was the ghost of Christmas present. You'll get there when you read the book. Or see one of the many movies based on the book. My favorite is the 1971 musical, *Scrooge.* The actor portraying me was spot on."

"I'm only thirteen. That movie came out over fifty years ago. I didn't know they even made movies back then."

"Anyway," the giant smiled, "my curiosity helped me see into the heart of Scrooge."

"What did you see?" Clovor asked.

"I don't want to spoil it for Toby," the giant answered.

"The I stands for Insight," the giant continued, nodding to the compass.

"Insight? What is that and how do I get it?"

"Insight is knowing what to do with what you know. You will face some important decisions soon. Insight—taking what you know, combined with the wisdom of others, and your gut instinct—will guide you. Be smart when the moment comes."

A moment is coming? Was that an insight? Toby shivered.

"The S in Wise stands for Service: Be Kind. Do to others as you would have them do to you."

"Even to people like Clygon?"

"Yes, and people like your friend, Derrick."

"I wouldn't exactly call him my friend."

Toby scratched his nose.

"I'm not sure I can do that…"

"The E stands for Endurance: Be Resilient."

"I'm not quite sure what that means."

"Life is going to throw you challenges, Toby. Sometimes it will knock you down. Resiliency is the ability to get back up again… and again… and again. It takes work. It takes practice. It takes courage. But resilience will make you strong. And you're going to need it."

Toby shivered again.

He looked down at the compass. On his first visit, the HERO compass had guided him to draw a line in the sand. Perhaps this new compass would help him get the Sword back and defeat Clygon again. He put it in his pocket.

"And the second reason why you turned yourself into these ogres?" Toby asked.

"Where else should hope be, Toby, but in a place of despair?"

14

Do You See What I See?

They walked in silence for what felt like forever. The only noises were the scrunching of snow under their boots and the wind in the snow-covered trees. Light was beginning to brighten the sky. It was Mathilda who broke the quiet.

"Tell us about yourself, Sid."

"Um… okay… What do you want to know?"

"Have you and Toby been friends long?"

"We met a few months ago at school when a guy named Derrick kicked a chair out in front of Toby, causing Toby to fall and spill his lunch all over the floor. I was right behind him and tripped over him, and lost my lunch as well, so to speak."

He smiled at the memory.

"My mom, sister, and I had just moved to Minneapolis… Do you know where that is?"

Phoenix nodded his head, yes.

"Of course you do. You were wearing a Vikings parka. Anyway, we moved to Minneapolis from Hawaii when my dad was deployed overseas for a year."

"Wow," Phoenix said. "That's a change of weather."

"Used to it," Sid said. "We've moved a lot with my dad being in the army."

"You must be proud of him," Phoenix said.

"I am. Very. But I really miss him. He's only been gone a few months and we have several months to go." Sid let out a sigh.

"Why Minneapolis?" Mathilda asked.

"My mom's sister and her family live there."

More silence. More wind in the snow-covered trees.

"Do you have a last name?" Phoenix asked.

"Douglass."

"As in Frederick Douglass?" Mathilda asked.

Sid laughed. "My grandma likes to believe that we're related to him but we're not, at least not by blood."

More silence. More scrunching of the snow.

"Do you play..."

But Sid had stopped. He held up his right arm and pointed in front of him.

"Do you see it?" he asked.

About a half mile away the snow was... melting! Not just melting. It looked like, in about the length of two or three football fields, they would leave winter behind and enter into spring. In fact, it looked as if spring was moving toward them.

Mathilda and Phoenix exchanged glances.

They quickly headed forward, and as they did, they began to heat up. In a matter of minutes, the temperature rose several degrees until they finally had to shed their jackets. Even then they were still warm.

They stopped at the top of a hill looking down onto a running stream. To the right of the stream was an oval playing field. To the left—a hill with holes bored into it. To Sid's surprise, he saw elves walking in and out of them.

The trees along the stream were beginning to spring to life. Color broke out in splotches. They watched as one season transitioned to another right before their eyes.

"What's happening? Is that where you and Deckor first found us? Is that your home?" Sid asked, the questions tumbling out of him. *Do questions tumble?*

"It must be *Loach!*" Phoenix said. "It's bringing life back to *RiverHome!*"

Phoenix tore off down the hill path leading to the stream, with Mathilda and Sid behind him.

They quickly reached the stream and paused. Sid tried to take in the difference between now, with the emerging life and colors, and not that long ago when Plythar held a sword in his back and everything had been gray and lifeless.

His thoughts were interrupted by a shadow that passed over them followed by a loud squaaaaaawk!

A large bird, as in ginormous, landed in front of them. Sid backed away. He was terrified of birds. Even more than he was of clowns. *A raven? A blackbird?*

The bird ruffled its massive feathers and shook its head. As it did, the bird's head morphed into a human head with black hair, black eyebrows, and a black goatee.

Sid felt sick and horrified.

The bird-human head bowed slightly to Phoenix and Mathilda and then glanced at Sid.

It creeped him out.

Then… the bird-human head spoke. With… *an English accent?*

"Master Phoenix. Madame Mathilda. What a relief to see you both alive and well. You are well met. We heard rumors that Clygon had captured you."

"The rumors are true, Hiriam. Clygon captured Thomas, the Healer, Donold, and Deckor along with the ogre, Oreea. We managed to escape with Sid here."

They all looked at Sid and saw the terror in his eyes. And they all started to laugh.

"Forgive us," Mathilda said. "We forget that those of you on the other side of the portal have never met a drone before."

"A drone?" Sid asked.

"Yes, a drone. Sid, this is Hiriam. He is the captain of our friends, the drones. Hiriam, this is Sid, friend of Toby Baxter."

Hiriam bowed his bird-human head to Sid and said, "It is an honor to meet you, Sir Sid, friend of Toby Baxter."

"Um… ah… likewise," muttered Sid, still a bit woozy in the stomach.

Hiriam turned his attention back to Phoenix and Mathilda.

"Because of the weather, we've been grounded for a while. But with the thaw, we've started our reconnaissance flights again. Nothing to report as of yet, I'm afraid, except that the replacement sword—*Loach*—is glowing. As you might surmise, that *Loach* is glowing is a good thing because it's putting life back into the land. On the other hand, it also might mean…"

"That war is coming… again," Mathilda finished the thought, shaking her head.

"War?" Sid gulped. He didn't sign up for this.

"Not to worry, Sir Sid, friend of Toby Baxter," Hiriam said. "A new sword is here. Toby Baxter is here. You're here." But Hiriam didn't seem all that confident about the addition of Sid. "I will report back to you at dinner time."

"Thanks, friend," Phoenix said.

Hiriam shook his head, turning it back into a bird head and flew off.

Squaaaaaawk!

Sid wanted to gag.

Phoenix patted him on the back.

"I'm hungry. I'm guessing you are too, although you look a little green. I'm assuming Grandma is back home. And she's a great cook!"

Just as Phoenix was about to move, Sid spoke up.

"The sword you keep talking about?"

"*Loach?*" Mathilda asked.

"Is that its name?"

"It's Celtic for hero."

"It's just that… it was glowing when we went to bed, and when I woke up, Toby was gone and so was his sword. Other than that, I know nothing about it or why it's important."

"So let's go see it in action!" Phoenix said as he quickly headed up the stream.

"But I thought we were going to eat?" Sid called after him.

Mathilda grabbed his arm. "There's no stopping him now. We'll eat afterward."

As they walked along the path, they could see the tree leaves gaining more color. It must have been about seventy degrees by now and Sid was hot. But as he turned a corner, he was met by a refreshing mist of water from a waterfall up ahead. To their right, in front of the falls, was the big tree log leading to the other side of the stream. That path seemed to stop at the face of the cliff wall.

Sid looked around. He'd been here before, he knew it. Not here here as in this land. But here as in a place just like this back home. He just couldn't find it in his brain.

"It's through a portal in that cliff wall over there where you and Thomas came," Mathilda said. "And over here…"

They all heard it at the same time. A low, deep buzzing sound. It vibrated underneath them. It seeped into their souls. But there was something about the buzzing. It seemed distressed. It seemed to be signaling… a warning?

"It's *Loach!*" Phoenix said, and dashed up a path to his left. Mathilda followed him and Sid followed her.

The buzzing grew louder and more desperate. Sid could see something glowing up ahead. A reddish glow. A few steps later, the sword came into view.

Life surged all around it. Sid could feel it. He could hear it. He could see it. He took a few tentative steps closer, not wanting to be burned by its glow. And that's when he noticed something carved in the monument that held the sword.

I.C.E. Call Toby Baxter.

"What does that mean?" Sid asked. But neither Phoenix nor Mathilda were paying attention to him. Their eyes were glued to the sword as they walked around it.

"*Loach* is obviously working its magic," Mathilda said, "but something is wrong. It's trying to tell us something."

As Phoenix and Mathilda studied *Loach*, Sid continued to move closer to it. But that wasn't quite right. *Loach* was drawing him. Almost dragging him. Sid couldn't stop himself. Before he knew it, he was standing on the monument.

"Sid!" Mathilda screamed. "Don't…"

But it was too late. Sid put his hands on the hilt of *Loach*, and as he did, his body stiffened and his head flew back. Wind and noise and buzzing and light surrounded him physically and mentally. He saw things. Frightening, fragmented images raced across his mind. He could feel burning in his hands.

And then it all went silent. Deathly silent.

Loach let go of him—that's the only way he could describe it later. He fell backwards into the arms of Phoenix and Mathilda. He was exhausted.

"They're… Toby… Thomas… your friends… they're…" Sid began to shake uncontrollably.

"What, Sid! What did you see?" Phoenix was yelling at him.

But Sid had passed out.

15

A Wonderful Christmas Time

Judah covered his ears. He tried to hum over the noise. He tried to go to a happy place. But… he… couldn't… get… the song… out of his… head. Drummer and his nineties cover band had just finished playing *Last Christmas* by Wham!

He bonked himself on the head, trying to dislodge the song from his brain.

"At least," he said to himself, "they didn't play…"

And as if on cue…

Wonderful Christmas Time by Wings came blasting from the band.

"Ahhhhhh…" Judah screamed as he covered his ears and ran out of the cave for some peace and quiet.

Jerry joined him a few moments later. The two of them stood in silence, covered by the hush of the snow.

"Of all the Christmas songs ever written…" Judah let the thought hang in the air.

"It works like an Echo Egg doesn't it?" Jerry replied.

Judah turned to Jerry. "I've heard of them but have never actually seen one."

"We use them only when necessary. A last resort if you will. Throw one of those eggs onto the ground and it explodes with an irritating song that bores into your mind like an earworm. It can take days for it to work its way out of the system. I used one once and forgot to put on my earmuffs. I was humming Morris Albert's "Feelings" for three straight days!"

Just then Drummer joined them.

"Speaking of earworms…" Jerry whispered.

"What did you think of my band, Judah?"

Jerry stifled a laugh as Judah choked on a reply. "It was… um… ah… yah… it… was… yup. And on top of that, you are one fantastic drummer."

"Thanks!" Drummer seemed genuinely pleased.

They stood for a few moments, taking in the silence, or, in Judah's case, trying to get the songs out of his head.

"Something's bothering me," Judah said, the Echo Egg in his mind clearing. "Are you sure we can trust Plythar? Something about him just doesn't feel right."

"It's hard to let go of old hatreds, isn't it?" Drummer smiled. "But look at me. I like you and you're a smelly river elf!"

"Smelly river elf!" Judah muttered. He had been breathing through his mouth since Plythar introduced him to Drummer. That distinctive troll smell gagged him every time he accidentally breathed through his nose.

"Besides," Drummer continued. "He rescued you from the trolls. He led you to me. And as I understand it, he's done the same for some of your friends. So, yes, I'd say you can trust him."

"I've been with this group for several weeks on and off, Judah. You can trust them too," Jerry added.

"But can we really trust Plythar?" Judah asked himself as they headed back inside.

The cave was a beehive of activity. Trolls, gnomes, and ogres huddled over maps, preparing weapons, taking naps, practicing offensive and defensive moves. Judah moved to a corner not sure what he should do, still on high alert. He had an uneasy feeling about all of this. His sister would tell him he always had an uneasy feeling about things.

Jerry, followed by Saaba, brought him a hard roll of bread and some water.

"How do you recruit these people?" Judah asked. "How can you be sure you can trust them?"

"We can't. But the only way people end up here is if someone brings them along. So we have to believe that everyone here has the same goal—to defeat whatever plan Clygon has and to build a new peace. We may not have always gotten along with each other, and when this is over we may go back into our corners. But for now, we all have a common goal. To put Clygon back where he belongs."

Someone called Jerry's name. Jerry grabbed Judah by the arm and led him to a large table. On it were maps with lots of lines on them, all leading to *Ogreton Heights.*

"We believe Clygon is planning his final showdown here. You probably already know that that's where the giant is being held."

Judah couldn't take it any more. He whispered to Jerry, "You wouldn't happen to have some menthol that I can put under my nose? If I take one more sniff of those trolls, we're going to have the contents of Judah's stomach to deal with."

Jerry laughed so loud everyone around him went silent. He apologized and slipped away for a moment, returning with a cup of peppermint hot chocolate.

"Drink this. It should help," Jerry said.

Judah took a sip when the hairs on the back of his neck stood up. He turned and found himself face to face with Plythar.

Everyone stopped.

"Hello, friends," Plythar said.

But there was nothing friendly in how he said it.

16

Sing a Christmas Carol

"Once upon a time of all the good days in the year, upon a Christmas eve, old Scrooge sat busy in his counting house. It was cold, bleak, biting, foggy weather; and the city clocks had only just gone three, but it was quite dark already."

Toby heard the voice of his grandfather coming to him from a deep sleep…

"The door of Scrooge's counting house was open, so that he might keep his eye upon his clerk, who, in a dismal little cell beyond, a sort of tank, was copying letters. Scrooge had a very small fire, but the clerk's fire was so very much smaller that it looked like one coal."

Toby opened his eyes. Apparently, he had fallen asleep. He looked up and saw that the giant was reading to him from an old book: *A Christmas Carol* by Charles Dickens, the same book his mom wanted him to read.

"'A merry Christmas, Uncle! God save you!' cried a cheerful voice. It was the voice of Scrooge's nephew, who came upon him so quickly that this was the first intimation Scrooge had of his approach."

He noticed Clovor leaning on her arm, listening to the story…

"'Bah!' said Scrooge, 'Humbug!'

"'Christmas a humbug, Uncle! You don't mean that, I am sure?'

"'I do. Out upon merry Christmas! What's Christmas time to you but a time for paying bills without money; a time for finding yourself a year older, and not an hour richer; a time for balancing your books and having every item in 'em through a round dozen of months presented dead against you? If I had my will, every idiot who goes about with "Merry Christmas" on his lips should be boiled with his own pudding, and buried with a stake of holly through his heart. He should!'"

The giant shut the book and set it on his ample stomach. He smiled down at Toby and Clovor.

"Isn't that wonderful writing?" the giant asked.

"Wonderful? It sounds pretty nasty to me… at least what I could understand of it," Toby said. "Boiling people in their own pudding! Burying people with a stake of polly through their hearts…"

Clovor laughed. "It's holly, Toby. You know, the little red berries on green leaves you put up on a Christmas tree or over your fireplace?"

"Still. Sounds horrible," said Toby. "Doesn't seem all that Christmasy! Why do you like this story so much?"

The giant looked down at them for several moments, until Toby started to feel uncomfortable.

"What? What is it?" Toby asked.

At that moment, the door to the cell swung open. Oreeo walked in, sword in his hand, nose plug firmly in place, his eyes a bit glazed.

"Must be the drug," Clovor whispered to Toby.

"Up against the wall!" he shouted at them.

As Toby got up and moved back, he could see several armed guards standing outside the door.

"You!" Oreeo said, pointing his sword at the giant. "I want you to move very slowly out of that door and follow the guards."

Toby moved toward Oreeo but Clovor caught him by the arm.

"Where are you taking him?" Toby demanded, anger ready to explode out of him.

"Toby," the giant said in his grandpa's voice. "It's okay. It's almost time."

"Time for what?" Toby asked, fear zinging through him.

But the giant didn't answer. Instead, he leaned down to Toby and Clovor and breathed on them. It was a long, slow exhale that engulfed the two of them. Though neither said anything, they could both feel something stirring in their souls. A sense of urgency… a sense of caution… and ultimately, a sense of hope.

Toby didn't see it but Clovor did. The longer the giant exhaled, the paler he became. The color seemingly drained from his entire being, including his clothes. She stifled a cry as she didn't want to draw attention to herself or to the giant, whatever it was he was doing.

"Be WISE, Toby," the giant said with one last breath. "And 'Think Scrooge' when the moment comes."

"'Think Scrooge?' What does that mean? What are you talking about?"

The giant moved his eyes toward the book now on the floor. Clovor followed them and nodded.

Out of breath and worn out from the effort, the giant dragged himself through the cell door, but not before offering a small smile to Oreeo and a nod of his head to the guards in the hallway.

Oreeo turned, put the tip of his sword just below Toby's chin, and said, "We have a surprise for you, Toby Baxter. And this time there will be no line in the sand."

Oreeo found that hilarious and laughed as he slammed the cell door shut behind him. "I'll be back for you soon, hero. And for you too, small elf woman."

17

Winter Wonderland

Judah, Jerry, Drummer, and the others in the Resistance—trolls, ogres, and gnomes, about twenty-five in all—followed Plythar out of the cave. Judah sighed when he saw what awaited them: Donold, Deckor, the Healer, and Blythar. He was surprised to see Thomas Baxter. But what captured his attention was a stunningly beautiful ogre warrioress. When her eyes met his, he felt electricity radiate from his heart to his head, his hands, and his feet. She noticed, raised an eyebrow at him, and smiled. More electricity. *What's going on?* He shook his head. *This was no time for… for… for whatever that just was.*

Then he saw Clygon. He looked about the same as the last time when they were in Clygon's stronghold with Toby: blubbery, a huge wart on his oversized nose, blood-vein-rippled ears, and the same frightening, menacing look that turned the bowels of lesser people to water.

"Well. Well. Well. The gang's all here. Or almost all. We're short a few river elves who, I'm sure, will find their way to us.

"And not long from now, we'll catch up to a few of our more endearing friends, like young Toby Baxter…"

Judah turned to Deckor and mouthed, "Toby is here?"

Deckor nodded yes.

"…and your sister I believe it is, Judah," Clygon continued, "Rose is it? Daffodil? Sunflower? Lavender? Petunia? Fungus?…"

"It's Clovor and she's my sister," Deckor said defiantly. "And I'm pretty sure that, when this is done, you won't forget her name."

"Whatevs, as the kids say," Clygon responded with a menacing laugh. "Unfortunately for you, we're ready for you this time, I'm afraid. We've spent the last few years preparing for this moment, haven't we, Plythar?"

Plythar nodded, moved behind the Resistance group and herded them toward the other prisoners. Judah fist-bumped Deckor and nodded at

Thomas. Blythar tried to shrink out of view, confused as to what game his brother was playing. The Healer stood silently, taking in the scene. Donold grunted.

Judah ended up next to the ogre warrioress. His hands instantly went clammy. His heart started to race. He could feel his face turn red. *What in the world?*

"My name's Oreea," she whispered into his ear. That was it. Judah was officially gobsmacked.

"My name's ah… um… it's… ah…"

"This is my cousin, Judah," Deckor whispered to Oreea. "He's got quite the way with words, doesn't he?" He bumped Judah with his shoulder and laughed.

Judah recovered himself enough to slide over to Thomas. "When did you get here?"

Before Thomas could answer, Clygon began yelling out orders. "To demonstrate my benevolent magnificence…"

"Do you even know what those words mean?" Deckor sneered, only to be butted on the side of his head by a sword handle. Donold made a move toward the troll who'd hit Deckor but thought the better of it and merely grunted.

"As I was saying," barked Clygon, "to demonstrate the goodness and honor of the trolls—and, by trolls, I mean those who remained loyal to me," he added, giving a stink eye to the trolls in the Resistance, "we won't tie you up. But if you try to escape, if you step out of line, we won't come after you. We'll simply lop off the head of your friend, Thomas here."

Clygon looked them all in the eyes to make sure they understood the ground rules. Donold added another grunt.

"Righty oh, then. Plythar, how about you take the lead? You three trolls take up the rear. And you four trolls, surround me and keep me safe! The rest of you, keep your eyes on this group. We'd hate for any of them to miss out on the big party we have planned."

The snow had started falling again. Heavy snowflakes, making it hard to see. The forest and the dark clouds didn't help.

"Magnanimous one," Deckor sneered, his head still throbbing. "Might I ask where we are headed?"

Clygon replied, "I guess there's no reason why you can't know. There's no one left to rescue you. We're headed to *Ogreton Heights*."

"And what might the plans be once we get there?" Deckor dared to ask.

Clygon laughed. "I don't want to give away the ending but here's a tease for you if you will: It will be an ending!"

Clygon, Plythar, and the troll soldiers broke out into laughter, patting themselves on the back and goading their prisoners on through the snow with their swords.

"Oh, and by the way, if you're hoping for a Toby Baxter-type ending like last time, remember, I have the Sword! And this time around, it's not working. On the fritz, you might say. Now, no more interruptions. We have a schedule to keep."

They walked through the snow in silence, all of them lost in their thoughts, some of them plotting how to get out of this mess.

Drummer made his way up to Judah, Deckor, and Thomas. After introductions were made, Drummer asked, "So, what's the plan?"

"What plan?" Deckor asked.

"Exactly!"

"Exactly what?"

"What's the plan? I've heard the Baxter stories enough to know there's always a plan."

"No plan," Judah muttered.

Oreea tripped and bumped into him. Chills ran up and down his spine. *Get control of yourself, Judah!*

"Don't worry, little drummer troll," she said, regaining her balance. "This story isn't done yet. Is it, Judah?" She winked at him. Judah almost fell over. *Knock it off, Judah. This is a war, not a Taylor Swift song.*

Jerry managed to make his way up to the front of the prisoners. Because he was so short he had to run to keep up.

Without saying anything, he caught Judah's attention. Then Deckor's. Then Oreea's, and Thomas's, and Donold's and Blythar's. And finally, Drummer's. He motioned his head to the right, up the hill. Slowly, they all turned their eyes that way and saw the big, green eyes of Saaba the wolf. The wolf nodded at them and then was gone.

***

The torches carried by the troll soldiers pierced the darkness enough to enable them to see a few feet ahead at a time. After several hours they stopped to rest. The prisoners were allowed to answer the call of nature under guard. Surprisingly, they had the decency to give Oreea some privacy. Or maybe it was the raised eyebrow she gave one of the troll soldiers that warned him to back off.

The snow was fresh enough to be used for hydration. The torches helped them ensure the snow was white, not yellow.

"Toby brought *Loach*," Thomas whispered to Judah, Jerry, and Drummer as the guards took the opportunity to relieve themselves.

Judah smiled. "That's great news. Clygon doesn't know?"

"It doesn't sound like it."

"Shhh…" Deckor said. He nodded his head to the left.

Plythar emerged out of the darkness. "If you keep talking about it, he will know. Now keep your mouths shut!"

As Plythar walked away Judah said, "I don't trust that troll. No offense, Blythar."

"None taken. Well… some taken. But until he shows us otherwise, I'm going to assume he's on our side," Blythar said. "What else can we do?"

"Exactly!" Drummer said.

Donold grunted.

After a thirty-minute rest stop, they were back on their feet. The miles seemed to drag on and on. It was hard to tell if they were making any progress.

But then, the snow began to ease up, enough for them to see in the distance the lights of *Ogreton Heights.*

Clygon stopped for a moment forcing the rest of them to do the same.

The lights illuminated the snow around the fortress. The stars above encircled it with a web of tiny lights. The deep silence of the forest created by the snow added to the magic.

"It's beautiful," Oreea whispered in Judah's ear.

"Yes, you are," he said to himself—he thought—but Deckor giggled and said, "You're worse than Phoenix when he first met Roxie. Get a grip."

"Quite a sight, isn't it?" Clygon fake-sighed. "A perfect place for torture, mayhem, revenge, and death."

"A veritable winter wonderland," Judah muttered.

Donold merely grunted.

18

I Heard the Bells...

Sid was chewing on his first big bite of a footlong hotdog, smothered in ketchup, mustard, sweet relish, onions, and sauerkraut. That footlong was the best part of attending a baseball game. Well, almost the best part. The best part was being at Target Field with his dad, watching the Minnesota Twins beat up on the Arizona Diamondbacks with Toby and Mr B sitting next to them. Then, again, as he took a second big bite of that hotdog, maybe that hotdog was...

Humming interrupted him. Subtle, but powerful. That Celtic *Lord of the Rings*-type music. It reached deep down into his soul.

"Sid... I need you to show me what you saw when you held *Loach*. I'm here with you. You'll be okay. Can you let me in? It's important."

It was the river elf grandma. *How did she get into my mind? Where am I?*

When Phoenix and Mathilda carried the unconscious Sid into their *RiverHome* house, Grandma met them in the hall. She immediately took control.

"Get him into Toby's bedroom."

"What are we going to do?" Phoenix yelled over his shoulder. "The Healer has been taken by Clygon."

Grandma didn't answer. She headed into her bedroom, and moments later, entered Toby's bedroom, wearing a red shawl.

Both Phoenix and Mathilda looked at her with shock and awe.

"We didn't... are you... how long have you..." Mathilda couldn't find the words.

Grandma moved over to Sid, whose body was stretched out on Toby's bed, taut and in obvious distress.

"No time right now. Yes, I am a Songstress, assistant to the Healers. Long since retired. But I'll have to do."

Grandma placed her left hand on Sid's forehead and grabbed his hand with her right. She began with a low hum, her eyes looking him over, attempting to read what his body was trying to say.

Phoenix quickly explained what had happened at the monument.

Grandma nodded and continued to hum. She closed her eyes and spoke to Sid's subconscious.

"Sid, can you show me the images you saw?"

But Sid didn't want to go back there. Instead, he found himself standing in front of Keeah. She was sort of his girlfriend in Hawaii before his family moved to Minneapolis. On their last day together, he leaned in for the first time and kissed her. It was awkward. It was embarrassing. It was magical. And... *what am I doing? I don't want Grandma to see this!*

Phoenix and Mathilda noticed a smile growing on Grandma's face. She looked up at them. "A girl," she whispered.

Phoenix turned to Mathilda with a look that said, What does a girl have to do with any of this? Mathilda simply shrugged.

Try as he might, Grandma was able to ease down his defenses, and now, he is standing with his hands on Toby's sword. Instantly, the images flood his mind... a hollowed-out castle or cathedral of some sort... snow and wind swirling inside of it... fires from torches casting ominous shadows... the screeching of animals in the distance... three unicorns off to the right neighing in terror, ropes around their necks held by trolls... a gray, lifeless giant discarded in a corner... Thomas Baxter, legs and arms extended and tied, making him look like a human X... Toby on his knees... Clygon mocking him ... broken pieces of something metallic at Clygon's feet... A nod from Clygon to an ogre who took out his sword and moved toward Toby... all of this he saw, as if hovering above the scene...

His body jerked as he tried to run from the pictures in his mind.

The humming grew louder.

"Sid," Grandma hummed. "Sid. It's okay. I'm here."

She could sense Sid relaxing just a bit.

"Sid, I want you to look again..."

Immediately Sid tensed. He couldn't do it again. Now he's sliding off the roof of Toby's house...

"Sid, you must. I need to see those images clearly."

For a second time, Sid gave in to the humming. Grandma and Sid watched the images again right up to the point where the ogre neared Toby with his sword.

"Stay here a moment, Sid."

Sid's body fought her.

"Sid, I'm with you. You are not in any danger."

Somehow, Grandma took control of the images. She paused on this one and then moved on to that one. Almost like freezing a picture on an iPad or TV screen. She moved her attention to the fringes of Sid's vision. Concentrating. Searching. Then she saw it. Sid didn't. But Grandma did. A shadow with light radiating out of it. And she smiled to herself.

"Sid," she hummed to him, "*Loach* sought you out for a reason. It's speaking to you. These are but images, shadows, of things that might be. Thomas, Toby, my grandchildren, our friends, are in deep trouble. But you, Sid, you have an important role to play. This is not the end of the story. You can—you will—help write the ending."

Sid's body began to relax. In his subconscious, he asked, "How?"

"That, young Sid, will be answered in due time. Now," Grandma pulled something out of her pocket. "Do you want to go back to the scene with your girlfriend or do you want to fall into a deep sleep? Personally, I'd like to see what happened with the two of you."

Sid instead went back to the hotdog.

"I thought as much," Grandma hummed. "I want you to slow your breathing. That's it. Good. Now, Sid, relax your body. Unlock your fists. Let your legs, arms and shoulders go limp. Good. Listen to my humming... Yes. Good. Now, when I ring the bell, I want you to fall into a deep, healing sleep."

Grandma sounded the small bell that had been in her pocket. She let the sound fade. Then she rang it again. And then a third time.

Within minutes, Sid was in a deep, dreamless sleep.

Several moments later, Grandma stopped humming and removed her hands from him.

Mathilda and Phoenix looked at her, their faces asking the question, well...?

"He'll be all right. He needs some rest. Then he'll need a good river elf meal."

"But what did he see?" Mathilda asked.

"He saw his place in this story," Grandma said cryptically.

After Grandma walked out of the room, Mathilda said to Phoenix, "Did you know she was a Songstress?"

"Nope," Phoenix said as he plopped down into a bean bag chair next to Sid's bed, promptly falling asleep.

"How does he do that?" Mathilda whispered to herself.

She took one more look at Sid. She could see his slow, even, deep, breathing. She could also hear Phoenix's snoring and hoped it wouldn't wake Sid. She closed the door behind her and headed off to ask Grandma if she had any more secrets she might want to share.

***

Sid!

Deep in the recesses of his mind, he heard a voice calling to him. A voice different from Grandma's. Not quite human. Then he heard buzzing. Deep. Urgent.

Sid! It's your time.

His eyes flew open. He stared at the ceiling above him, no idea where he was. He heard gentle snoring next to him. Phoenix. Sound asleep.

Sid sat up. He kicked the bean bag where Phoenix slept. In one move, Phoenix opened his eyes, jumped out of the bean bag, grabbed his sword, and looked around. His eyes landed on Sid.

"Sid. What is it?"

"*Loach.* It's calling me. It's calling us. We have to go."

19

Carol of the Bells

Toby paced back and forth in the cell as Clovor sat curled up in a corner reading the book left by the giant.

"What did he mean, 'Think Scrooge' when the time comes? What time? And how is my thinking about Scrooge going to help?"

Clovor simply answered with, "Mm… mm."

He paced some more.

"I don't have the Sword. I have no idea what 'Think Scrooge' means. Once again, I'm completely out of my depth…"

He stopped and looked down at Clovor.

"You're not being very helpful. You're the commander of the river elves. What are we supposed to do? What am I supposed to do?"

He could feel the fear overwhelming him. *I'm still just a kid!*

Without looking up, Clovor said, "I'm looking for clues in this book. When the giant said, 'Think Scrooge,' he motioned with his eyes toward this book. So, a bit of peace and quiet would be helpful about now."

"Why does it always have to be about books?" Toby muttered.

"Here, listen to this: Scrooge is visited by his old partner, Jacob Marley, who's been dead for seven years. He's come to warn Scrooge to change his ways or Scrooge will end up in the same situation as Marley, wandering the afterlife in heavy chains."

"This Christmas book just gets cheerier and more cheerier," Toby said, as he sat down next to her.

"You don't add the word *more* before an -er word," she said without looking up.

"Huh?"

"So Marley tells Scrooge he's going to be haunted by three spirits—or ghosts, as we called them earlier—in order, I guess, to knock some sense or goodness into him…"

But Toby was no longer paying attention.

"Do you see that?"

"See what?"

Toby got up and moved to the wall where the giant had been leaning moments earlier. A small splotch of orange poked out from a little pile of hay. As Toby moved closer, he also saw bits of blue and red. He brushed away the straw and turned to show Clovor three colored eggs. But it wasn't the eggshells that were colored. The actual eggs themselves were orange, blue, and red.

"Are these Easter eggs?" Toby asked.

Clovor put down the book and walked over to Toby. She took the orange egg and cradled it in awe. It had a squeeze-ball feel about it.

"Toby," she whispered. "These are Ostern eggs…"

"Don't tell me. The E in Eostern is silent…"

Clovor shook her head. "Ostern Egg doesn't start with a silent E, Toby. Where do you get this stuff?"

"But… Eogre Eggs starts with a silent E!"

"This is an egg of a different color, Toby."

"What? Never mind. What does this egg do?"

"The ancient myths tell us that the giants curated these eggs over the centuries to be used only in extraordinary circumstances. I didn't know they still existed. The Christmas Giant must have left them for us."

"What kind of circumstances?"

"The giants were opposed to violence unless it was the last resort. They created these eggs to diffuse violence when possible, in the hope of turning enemies into friends."

"Can you eat them?"

But Clovor was focused on the egg. "Can I see the other two?" she asked.

She took the blue and red eggs and examined them up close.

"Look at this, Toby. Do you see…"

"Look at what?" They hadn't heard the ogre soldier enter the cell. "What do you have there?"

Clovor quickly put her hands behind her back to hide the eggs while Toby stepped in front of her.

"She was just showing me… ah… um… how to make shadow animals with my hands."

Clovor groaned.

"Uh huh. Let me see what you have," he demanded. "Now!"

Clovor stepped out from behind Toby and revealed the three eggs.

The ogre's eyes widened.

"Are those… are those… Ostern eggs?"

Clovor nodded, yes.

"That's Ostern with no silent E at the beginning of it," Toby added helpfully.

The ogre looked back at the cell door, pulled out his sword, and pointed it at Toby's stomach.

"Listen to me carefully. I don't have much time. My name is Buddeeo but everyone calls me Buddy. I'm part of the Resistance. There are several of us here working undercover. Hope caught us just in time, thanks to the giant. Clygon will be here soon…"

The troll shuddered. As did Clovor. As did Toby.

"The grand hallway is set up for his visit and you are to be his guests of honor."

"Been there, done that," Toby muttered.

"We are outnumbered but we will do what we can to help you against Clygon. However, you need to know that the odds are not on our side."

A throat cleared itself by the cell door. Oreeo! How much had he heard?

"Soldier! May I ask what's going on here?"

Buddy, his sword still pointed at Toby's stomach, said, "I brought them their dinner, as you ordered," nodding his head toward a tray of food by the door. "This one here," he pointed at Toby, "was refusing to eat. I thought he needed a bit of convincing. I know you will want him at full strength for the reception you've got planned." He laughed. Oreeo joined him.

Then Oreeo turned serious.

"Leave us."

Buddy sheathed his sword and turned his back to Toby and Clovor, and headed out of the cell. But not before Clovor slid him the Ostern eggs.

Oreeo walked up and put his face within inches of Toby's face. His breath smelled of fish and mushrooms. Toby could feel himself turning green.

"I don't know what the two of you think you're up to…"

He paused.

Then he burped into Toby's face.

Toby's knees buckled but Clovor caught him just in time.

"…but, whatever it is, enjoy it now. Tonight is your last night here. Or anywhere, for that matter."

He turned as if to walk out the cell door but rounded back to them.

"Oh… and by the way, our guests have arrived. And we have a new surprise for you, Toby Baxter!"

With that, he walked out, kicking the food tray over.

***

They stood still for several moments, making sure Oreeo was really gone. Toby moved over to the food now spread over part of the cell floor. He was able to salvage the bread rolls and beef jerky. The water, unfortunately, was watering the floor.

The two of them ate in silence. Sort of. Toby could actually hear Clovor's brain thinking.

She picked up the book and started reading.

But Toby felt something buzzing in his pocket. It was the compass. He took it out and watched as the arrow spun around from W to I to S to E again and again…

…he was back standing in front of Clygon in Clygon's stronghold. The events of that moment flashed through his mind… seeing his friends led out onto the field… Mathilda left half-dead… the blood-red anger that surrounded him… the spinning of the HERO compass…. the words and images that guided him… drawing the line in the sand…

You've been here before, Toby. Be WISE. Be a HERO…

"Toby," Clovor's voice came from far away. "I don't think it's a coincidence that the giant left us the book and three Ostern eggs."

Toby looked around trying to get his bearings. The compass had stopped compassing or whatever it was doing.

"How long have I been asleep?"

"You weren't asleep. Pay attention. What's wrong with you! Now, think about it. Scrooge is visited by three ghosts—the ghost of Christmas past… the ghost of Christmas present… and the ghost of Christmas yet-to-come. Three ghosts. Three eggs. What do you think?"

"Huh?" he answered, trying to wake up his brain. "Is this a conundrum? A riddle? Anything helpful or useful?"

"Sorry, I left out one small, but important detail. You probably didn't notice but each of the eggs had a small symbol on it. The orange egg had a

98

small triangle, the red egg had two connected triangles, and the blue one had three connected triangles. Past. Present. Future."

"Okay… so what?"

"So, what if…" Clovor continued.

At that moment four things happened at once.

Both Toby and Clovor felt an immediate, deep sense of overwhelming loss, so painful both began to weep.

Bells started to ring throughout *Ogreton Heights.*

An ogre soldier ran through the halls yelling, "The giant is dead! The giant is dead!"

The cell door opened and Oreeo walked in, followed by Plythar.

"It's party time! Plythar, care to do the honors?"

"Happy to, sir!"

With a big, menacing grin he moved toward Toby. The smell of vomit and sweat almost made Toby hurl. Plythar put a hand on his shoulder and whispered in his ear, "I'm going to pull my punch so act like I hit you in the stomach."

"What?"

But Plythar didn't pull his punch.

Epilogue

There's No Place Li...

Toby couldn't breathe. No matter how hard he tried to suck in air, nothing happened. He remembered falling off of a playground gym when he was a kid. He landed on his back, knocking the air out of him. It seemed like it had taken forever to recover his breath but it was probably only seconds.

This was different. He was sure Plythar's punch to the gut had gone all the way to his spine, completely popping his stomach. He was going to die here, in this cell, in *Ogreton Heights*.

But then the breath came. He gulped it as fast as he could. Big, large gasps of air that filled his lungs and his diaphragm. He never knew breath tasted so good.

Or hurt so much. The punch to his stomach had been deep and hard. Every breath caused him pain.

He realized then that he was curled up in a fetal position and that the cell floor felt remarkably... *cushy?*

He opened his eyes. The room was dark but a light in front of him caught his attention. It was his clock. On his nightstand.

He slowly turned to his right, looked down, and saw an empty sleeping bag. *Where is Sid?*

He felt a cold breeze blowing into his room from the direction of his closet. He was sure he felt snowflakes landing on him.

Then he heard a sound... *snoring?*... which drew his eyes to something glowing at the foot of his bed.

Author. Sound asleep. Sitting in Toby's desk chair. His head off to the side... his glasses askew... *askew?... wait... Author is sleeping... did I come up with that word on my own?*... on his nose. His notebook on his lap, about to slide off. A pencil in his left hand and a half-peeled multi-colored egg in his right. He was still wearing that extremely ugly Christmas sweater. And the Santa hat.

"Author! Wake up!"

Author jolted awake. His notebook, half-peeled egg, and glasses falling to the floor. He looked around, dazed. His eyes finally landed on Toby.

Toby? Is that you? What are you doing here?

"That's what I'd like to know. I think I've been knocked out of the story. The words are above your head."

Author looked up.

"Is this the Epigram? It can't be, can it? The story isn't over yet, is it? Unless you're playing some kind of mean trick and creating a cliffhanger."

Author picked up his notebook and scanned it, looking for something. He scratched his bald head under the Santa hat, picked up his pencil, and made a few notes.

This is really interesting, Toby. You're right. It's too early for the Epilogue—not Epigram by the way. Hmm... give me a minute...

Toby sat up gingerly.

"Ginger is an herb, right?" Toby asked, protecting his stomach with his arm.

Without looking up, Author said, The answer is, yes. But some refer to it as a spice. Or a person with red hair.

"I'm stating the obvious here, but if this isn't the Epilogue, I need to get back. What's happening? Why am I here?"

Well... I'm not sure. Something went wrong with the space-time continuum...

"The what?"

I think we're in the middle of an... let me think a moment... yes... I've got it. We're in the middle of an Excursus.

Excurses: O Tannenbaum

"An excursion? Like a cruise?"

Excurses. It means a digression in the story. For example, say you're writing a story about Christmas. You write a scene with a family around a Christmas tree and you decide to do an excurses, or digression, by providing a bit of history on how the Christmas tree came to be. You could write about the use and meaning of greens in ancient Rome and Egypt. You could include something on how the Germans lit up evergreens with candles and refer to the Christmas tree as a Tannenbaum...

"Author!"

Sorry. I guess I got caught in an excurses during your excurses.

"Author, I need to get back into the story. Now!"

Right. But here's the problem. As you know, time works differently in *RiverHome*. It's a...

"...timey-wimey thing. Yah. I know."

If we don't get you back into the exact part of the story where you left it, you could set off a chain reaction that would mess up the story.

"In what way?"

There could be two or more of you running around *RiverHome* at the same time!

"Like in *Spider-Man: No Way Home* where three Spider-Men from different universes team up?"

I was thinking more like Back to the Future...

"Huh?"

Marty McFly?... Dr Emmet Brown?... Biff Tannen?... Never mind. Give me a minute...

"Where's Sid?"

I can't tell you that, Toby. It would interfere with the story.

Toby watched as Author paged back and forth through his journal.

Okay, I think I've figured it out...

Author looked up and saw the hesitation in Toby's eyes.

What is it, Toby?

"Something bad was about to happen before I ended up here..."

Author nodded.

Take out your compass.

Toby reached into his pocket and pulled out the compass given to him by the giant. His breath caught as he remembered hearing the giant was dead. He looked at the coordinates: W-I-S-E.

Yes, Toby. Something bad is going to happen. Something that will challenge you to the core. Once again, you will be faced with the question: *How will you use your power?* **Once again, you will be tempted to meet violence with violence. Anger with anger. Despair with destruction. You'll need to be WISE, Toby. Remember what you saw in the last chapter...**

"The last what?..."

Um... remember what you saw in the cell when the compass started buzzing? You've been here before. Build on that. That's what endurance means. Start from a place of kindness and generosity, not anger or hatred. That's service. And be smart. Dig deep into what you've learned so far. That's insight...

"Why are you going backwards... E-S-I-W?"

To emphasize how important your starting point is. This time around, wonder will be your guiding light. Be curious, Toby! Now... let's get you back into the story...

Author turned a few pages in his journal and nodded.

"Is that an Easter Egg you're eating?"

Author ignored him.

So, here's what we're going to do. I'm going to read word-for-word what happened to you right before this excurses...

"You're going to read what?"

...As I do, you will walk through the closet to the portal. To make sure you land back at the exact point where you left the story I want you to take two steps, pause, and say to yourself, 'There's no place like *RiverHome.* **There's no place like** *RiverHome.'* **Then do it again. And then one more time. Hopefully, if we time it right, I will get to the end of the paragraph just as you get to the end of your closet and...**

"And?"

And you'll land back in the story, right where you were when Plythar punched you.

"Wait, what? I have to go through that again?"

Start walking, Toby. You have a story to finish.

Toby headed toward the closet door.

At that moment, Author read, four things happened at once.

Both Toby and Clovor felt an immediate, deep sense of overwhelming loss, so painful both began to weep.

Bells started to ring throughout *Ogreton Heights*.

Toby took two steps into the closet.

"There's no place like *RiverHome*. There's no place like *RiverHome.*"

An ogre soldier ran through the halls yelling, "The giant is dead! The giant is dead!"

The cell door opened and Oreeo walked in, followed by Plythar.

"It's party time! Plythar, care to do the honors?"

"Happy to, sir!"

Two more steps. "There's no place like *RiverHome*. There's no place like *RiverHome.*"

With a big, menacing grin he moved toward Toby. The smell of vomit and sweat almost made Toby hurl.

"There's no place like *RiverHome*. There's no place like *River...*"

Plythar put a hand on his shoulder and whispered in his ear, "I'm going to pull my punch so act like I hit you in the stomach?"

"What?"

But Plythar didn't pull his punch.

***

"Phew!" Author said to himself.

20

The Stars are Brightly Shining

"Where do you two think you're going in such a hurry?" It was Mathilda.

Sid slammed into Phoenix as Phoenix came to a screeching halt.

"Sid said that *Loach* is calling him. It's time, whatever that means."

Grandma walked over and put a hand on Phoenix's arm.

"We need to slow down a bit, boys. Let's take a breath, get our bearings, and above all, get something to eat. I'm not sending my heroes out hungry!"

"But Grandma…" Phoenix started to argue. But Grandma was already headed into the kitchen.

Phoenix, Mathilda, and Sid sat down at the table in the big hall as Grandma came out with a small meal of bread, cheese, and some elven ale.

The meal was interrupted by a knock on the door. Phoenix answered it and in flew Hiriam. He landed on a stand next to the table and turned his bird head into a human head. He and Phoenix talked quietly for several minutes, Phoenix becoming more animated.

Hiriam then turned his human head back into a bird head and flew outside. "Squaaaaaawk! See you at the monument! Squaaaaaawk!"

Phoenix turned around with a huge smile on his face.

"What was that all about?" Mathilda asked.

"You are gonna love this!" was all he said and ran down the hallway.

Grandma and Mathilda cleared the plates as Sid finished up his ale. Best drink he'd ever had.

Phoenix came back into the hall, his arms full of clothes.

"Here," he said to Sid, "put this on."

It was a Minnesota Vikings parka with the name, 'Page' written across the back shoulders.

"One of the great Purple People Eaters of the 1970s teams," Phoenix explained. But Sid already knew that. His dad had passed down the stories.

"Why this?" Sid asked.

"To give you some style, my young friend, as you save the world. And to keep you warm. It's going to be cold up there."

"Up where?"

"You'll also need this." He tossed a square-looking helmet with one small bar across the mouth area. It had a big yellow 'G' on it.

"No way," Sid said as he threw it back. "I. Will. Not. Wear. That. Thing. Whatever it is we're about to do, I'm not doing it with a Green Bay Packers helmet—and a throwback helmet at that—on my head. No way. Not happening."

Sid crossed his arms. He meant it.

Phoenix threw the helmet back at him. It hit Sid in the arms and plopped onto the floor.

"When you see how we're traveling, I'm pretty sure you'll wear anything on that noggin of yours," Phoenix said cryptically.

Sid muttered as he reached down for the helmet.

"So, what, if I may ask, is up?" Mathilda asked.

Phoenix quietly explained while Sid put on his parka. Unfortunately, the helmet fit perfectly. As Mathilda listened to Phoenix, her eyes grew wide and she began to giggle.

At that moment, Grandma walked in wearing what looked like latex gloves and holding a small vial in her hand.

"Sid, before you go, I'd like to give you a gift."

Sid looked at Phoenix and Mathilda, who both nodded and smiled.

"It's okay, Sid. You're going to like it, after a moment or two." Mathilda giggled again.

"Sid, could you kneel down in front of me?" Grandma asked.

Hesitantly, Sid knelt before her, but even on his knees, he still towered over her. Grandma poured a green-type liquid onto her right thumb, took Sid's right hand into her left, and then traced a line with the liquid from his wrist to his middle knuckle. He tried to pull his hand away as the whatever-it-was stung. But Grandma held tough.

By this time, Phoenix and Mathilda were next to him, humming another one of those Celtic melodies. As they did, Grandma said, "Sid, I mark you as a river elf. You are now one of us. Go in the knowledge that we are with you. Go in the power of your Creator. Be strong and courageous."

Sid looked at the line on his hand and remembered the green line on the hands of Toby and Mr B. *So that's where they got them.* Sid's line turned a darker shade of green due to his skin color, but it was the same mark. He suddenly felt shivers up and down his spine and a new sense of confidence. Everything had been so confusing up to this point. He had felt like he was simply along for the ride—by mistake. But now, the calling of the sword *Loach* and the mark of the river elves suggested that maybe he did have a role to play in this story.

As Sid was getting to his feet, Hiriam flew in. He changed to his human head and said, in that deep English voice, "They're here!"

"Woo hoo!" shouted Phoenix. "Let's go."

"Who's here?" Sid asked but Phoenix was already out the door right behind Hiriam, now with his bird head back on.

Mathilda gave Grandma a hug and grabbed her arrows and arrow-holding thingy… *her quacker… no… her quesadilla…no, that's not right either…*

"Quiver," Mathilda said.

"How did you know…"

"Elven magic!" she laughed.

Grandma hugged him.

"Go now, Sid. Your story is calling you! And remember, you are a river elf."

Sid stood there awkwardly, not sure how to respond, when Mathilda rescued him by pulling him toward the entrance to the outside.

It was dark. Mathilda grabbed a torch on the way out. As they rounded the corner toward the waterfall and *Loach,* they could see a torch bouncing up and down ahead. Phoenix!

"He's always in a hurry," Mathilda said. "But this time, for good reason."

"And that would be…?"

"You'll see very soon, Sid. I don't want to spoil the surprise."

"I think I've had enough surprises for a while."

They quickly made their way toward *Loach.* The waterfall sprayed mist on them as they turned left and headed up the hill. Sid could see something glowing through the trees, no doubt *Loach.* As they got closer, he could feel that buzzing again deep in his guts. And once again, he could feel the pull of Toby's sword, calling him, drawing him to it.

Phoenix was not alone. Off to the side, perched Hiriam with several other drones. Next to Phoenix were Roxie and a couple of gnomes.

"Roxie, what are you doing here?" Mathilda asked.

"I came to kiss Phoenix and then we're going to sit with Grandma and keep her company—and make sure she's safe, along with the rest of the river elves hiding in *RiverHome*. Demetrius here," she nodded toward another human-headed drone, "told us the plan and felt we'd be best used here."

The conversation began to blur as Sid found himself drawn deeper into the heart of the sword. *Loach's* buzzing increased, and its color grew gradually brighter and more intense. He knew he was supposed to grab hold of it, but after his last experience, he wasn't sure he was up for it.

Sid was now standing, once again, on the monument, his hands inches from *Loach's* hilt. Just as he was about to grab it, a gale-force wind hit from out of nowhere, threatening to blow them all away. He heard what sounded like helicopters above him.

Through the noise and the wind, he heard the others cheering. They were all looking up and so he did the same. His hands dropped to his side. His mouth fell so far open that he could have stuffed two full-sized Big Macs into it. And perhaps a large order of fries. Add in a vanilla milkshake… make that chocolate… *Why am I hungry again?… I just ate…*

Circling above them, lit by the glow of the torches and *Loach*, were three magnificent-looking flying dragons. *Duh. If they were circling above, of course, they would be flying dragons. What else would they be? And stop babbling in your mind, Sid.*

Finally, he was able to speak, sort of.

"Um… ah… what's the, ah… um…plan? And does this irritating Green Bay Packer's helmet have something to do with those dragons up there?" He wasn't sure if he was petrified or excited. Probably both.

The dragons landed and pulled in their wings.

"The plan, young Sid, as you can see, is *LOR*-worthy," said Phoenix.

"You know about *Lord of the Rings*?"

"Of course, we do. As I said earlier, we like to think of ourselves as distant cousins of the hobbits, or maybe even of Legolas and the elves."

"But that's just a story."

"Is it? Are you just a story? Is this just a story?"

That was too existential for Sid, whatever existential means.

"If Clygon wants a battle, then we're going to give him a battle. Jerry's wolf…"

"Jerry?" asked Sid.

"Sorry. Roxie's dad. Jerry's wolf, Saaba, just left with Saanti. They've gone to call their fellow wolves to *Ogreton Heights*. Hopefully, Judah and some of the Resistance will be there already."

"And these dragons, friend Sid," Mathilda said, "will be flying us there to deliver *Loach* to Toby." She giggled. "Sorry. I've never flown on a dragon before. This may very well be a first here in *RiverHome*! Toby met that dragon over there," she pointed to her left, "when he was last here. But you, Sid, get to fly with her."

The dragon bowed her head to Sid and... *did it wink her big yellow eye at him?*

Roxie gave Phoenix a big hug and a kiss and led her fellow gnomes back down the hill to the path to *RiverHome*. Hiriam, Demetrius, and the other drones returned to their bird heads, readying to join the air troops.

"What do I do now?" asked Sid. *I wish I had used the bathroom before we left.*

"Put the helmet on," Phoenix said.

"Seriously, do I have to? A Green Bay Packers helmet..." he muttered.

He shoved the helmet onto his head and then turned to *Loach*.

Once again, it drew him in. It glowed. It buzzed. It hummed. And it spoke: *Get me to Toby.*

Sid put his hands on the hilt and was immediately hit by a blast of energy that surged through his body. He held on... or maybe better said, *Loach* held on to him. Sid began to glow.

Phoenix and Mathilda stepped back, shielding their eyes. "Pull the sword out, Sid. We have to go," yelled Phoenix.

Sid gripped the hilt tighter and began to pull. Surprisingly, the sword slid out easily, and now, he was holding it above his head like an ancient Roman gladiator. Like Russell Crowe. Like Victor Mature. *Victor Ma-who?*

Once *Loach* was out of the monument, the energy, glow, and buzzing dissipated. Sid lowered it and looked over at the dragons. Phoenix and Mathilda were already sitting on theirs, hovering a bit off of the ground. Both of them laughing and whooping.

"How do I get onto mine with this sword?" But before they could answer him, the dragon reached out her wing, gently embraced Sid, and eased him just behind her head. Sid expected scaly skin, but her skin felt more like soft down feathers.

My name is Billie. He heard it in his mind. *The other two dragons are Ruphas and Dahrlah. Hang on.*

"Wait! What am I supposed to do with the sword when we get to Toby?"

"Trust *Loach,* Sid. Trust your dragon. And trust your gut instinct. You'll know what to do when we get there," Mathilda yelled.

Billie stretched out her wings, and before he knew it, Sid was high in the air. He could hear Phoenix and Mathilda laughing and woo-hooing. Sid, in the meantime, was holding on to the sword for dear life and grateful that, somehow, Billie was holding on to him.

Once his panic subsided, he took in the view. He'd never seen such bright stars before. He felt like he could reach out and touch them.

He repositioned the sword a bit in his hands so as not to drop it. As he did, he felt the mark seared into his right hand. Feeling a new sense of confidence, he held *Loach* above his head again and yelled, "Today… I'm a river elf. Let's do this!"

Then he leaned over and threw up.

21

Deck the Hall

Toby couldn't breathe. No matter how hard he tried to suck in air, nothing happened. He remembered falling off of a playground gym when he was a kid. He landed on his back, knocking the air out of him. It seemed like it had taken forever to recover his breath but it was probably only seconds. This was different. He was sure Plythar's punch to the gut had gone all the way to his spine, completely popping his stomach. He was going to die here, in this cell, in *Ogreton Heights.*

But then the breath came. He gulped it as fast as he could. Big, large gasps of air that filled his lungs and his diaphragm. He never knew breath tasted so good.

Or hurt so much. The punch to his stomach had been deep and hard. Every breath caused him pain.

He realized then that he was curled up in a fetal position… and suddenly, had a moment of déjà vu. *I already woke up from this in my… where was it…*

The conversation behind him brought him back to the moment, although conversation was too polite a word. Clovor was letting Plythar have it.

"You touch him again and I'll…"

"You'll what, little elf girl?"

Toby heard a smack. He looked up and saw Clovor's head snap back from a back-handed slap to her face from Plythar. She fell next to him, a big, bleeding cut on her cheek. He could see the tears that the slap had knocked out of her eyes.

He turned his head and noticed the small platter that had held their meager lunch. Without thinking, he grabbed it, sat up, and threw it like a frisbee at Plythar, hitting him smack in the forehead, knocking him backwards, leaving a huge gash with lots of blood. *Finally, I got to use one of my superpowers…*

Plythar regained his balance, wiped the blood out of his eyes, grabbed his sword and lunged at him. But Clovor quickly draped herself over Toby and held out her hand to take the blow of the sword.

"Enough!" Oreeo shouted.

Plythar stopped with the sword inches from Clovor and stepped back.

"You're going to rob Clygon of all of the fun, Plythar. And he won't like that. Now, put your sword away. Didn't your mom ever teach you that violence begets violence?"

Oreeo laughed at what he apparently thought was some kind of joke. Toby noticed that he seemed to do that a lot.

"And go wash that blood off of your face."

"This isn't done!" Plythar huffed as he left the cell.

Oreeo offered a hand up to Clovor but she refused it. She turned to Toby to see how he was doing.

Suddenly, Toby rolled over and puked. He was sure his stomach had imploded and would never be normal again.

They heard a commotion from somewhere down the hall. It was a combination of voices shouting, wolves growling, and metal clanging against metal.

"Ah… the rest of our guests have arrived just in time," Oreeo laughed again. "The more the merrier! Now, young Toby, let me get you some water to wash yourself off. You too, elf woman. The party is about to begin."

Fresh water was brought in and Toby and Clovor took turns washing, the blood in Clovor's case, and the vomit in Toby's case, off of themselves.

Two ogre soldiers walked in. One of them was Buddy.

"Let's tie them to each other," Oreeo said. "Just to make things interesting."

Buddy grabbed Toby's right hand and Clovor's left hand and tied them together with some sort of heavy-duty leather. It cut into their skin every time they tried to move.

"Okay, my friends. It's showtime!"

Buddy put the tip of his sword in Toby's back while Oreeo and the other ogre soldier led them out of the cell into a dark hallway, thankfully, lit by torches. Clovor squeezed Toby's hand.

As they moved down the hallway, they could hear music. *Music?* More specifically, badly-played Phil Collins music, Toby's dad's favorite singer. The drummer was actually pretty good but the rest of the band… *Are you suddenly Simon Cowell?*

As the music grew louder… and more grating… the temperature dropped. Snow started pelting them, and then, they found themselves outside, in what used to be… *a castle great hall? An old Abbey?* The walls were still up but the roof was gone, hence the cold and snow.

And if Toby wasn't about to have his head handed to him by Clygon, he would have been awed by the beauty and the majesty of the scene. Candle-lit evergreen trees. Big red and green balls. Christmas ornaments hanging off of green plants on the walls. The lights were made all the more dazzling by the falling snow. In the front, was a large stage lit up with candles and torches. It looked like a winter wonderland.

But then, both Toby and Clovor stopped.

Near the front, off to their right, they saw the other "guests." Clovor's legs buckled at the sight and this time Toby squeezed her hand.

Chained together, surrounded by troll and ogre guards were Judah, Deckor, Jerry, Donold—whose face had had a run-in with a troll or two—Blythar, the Healer, a tall, goddess-like ogre, and several trolls and ogres they didn't recognize. Next to them, were the three unicorns, tethered and held by a couple of ogres.

"I don't see Phoenix or Mathilda," whispered Clovor. "I hope this isn't like last time…"

Toby shivered.

On the other side of the hall, they saw Saaba, Saanti, and a pack of wolves, all tied down by their necks.

The sword in Toby's back prodded them further into the hall and that's when Toby saw him. The giant, his back against the wall near the front stage, gray and lifeless. Then Clovor saw him. And that was it. She began to weep. Toby joined her.

No Sword. No hope. Party over.

In the Air Tonight, played horribly by the band, jarred Toby out of his despair for a moment. He noticed that guards surrounded the band so, apparently, they were playing under duress. *That explained things, maybe.*

As the band wrapped up their terrible rendition of the song, the trolls and ogres loyal to Clygon began to chant his name. Cly-gon! Cly-gon! Cly-gon! They were ready for some action. So, too, apparently, was Oreeo.

"Elves and gnomes," came Oreeo's voice, amplified by the walls, "trolls and ogres, wolves and unicorns, welcome to *Ogreton Heights*!"

Loud cheering.

"I'd like to give a special nod to my sister, Oreea, who, for some reason, finds herself on the sideline with our enemies."

Amid the boos and hisses, Clovor said, "So that's who she is."

"Oreea, my sister, would you like to join me on stage for the events tonight?"

Oreea cleared her throat.

"I have no desire to have anything to do with you ever again, Oreeo. You are a traitor to your people. I prefer to stay here with my friends."

More booing, but this time a bit muted.

"As you wish. We all make choices and I'm not sure you've made a wise one. Oh well. Now, friends, it is my great pleasure to introduce to you tonight our host for this evening. You love him. You fight for him. You die for him. Put your hands together and welcome Clyyyyyyy-gawwwwn!"

The place again erupted into cheering and whooping.

The blubbery troll waddled onto the stage like an overaged rock star. He basked in the glory of the moment, his arms outstretched as if he were a god.

Clovor could feel Toby tensing. She looked at him and saw that he was beginning to radiate light—that same angry red light from the last time he stood before Clygon.

"Toby…" she whispered. But he was in another world. Good thing they were tied together.

Finally, Clygon raised his arms to quiet the crowd.

"Thank you, my good friend, Oreeo, and to all of the residents of this beautiful town. I am most honored to be here."

More cheers.

"But tonight is not about me…"

This time, laughter.

"Well, it's always about me, but tonight is also about my opportunity for a rematch with Toby Baxter…"

Boos and hisses.

"Bring him here, would you? I have a few gifts for you, Toby."

Toby and Clovor were marched up to the front of the hall, a few feet away from Clygon. But not far enough. The smell of sweat and vomit radiated off of the stage into their noses, their clothes, and their hair. Thankfully, Toby had vomited earlier. *Silver linings.*

"The last time young Toby Baxter and I went toe-to-toe he had an unfair advantage…"

Booing and hissing, along with a few cries of "cheater," thrown in.

"He had this!"

Clygon pulled out a bag, opened it, and poured out its contents onto the ground below the stage, in front of Toby and Clovor. It was the Sword. In pieces. Useless.

"We'll see just how powerful Toby Baxter is without his Sword, in a moment…"

Cheering and whooping.

"But I have one other gift for you, Toby, that I want to share with you, your friends, and the good people of *Ogreton Heights*."

But Toby wasn't paying attention. He felt something when the pieces of the Sword hit the ground. He felt the Sword's energy. He slowly reached out his hand and saw the Sword pieces begin to glow. It looked like they were actually starting to move together—reforming into the Sword—when a large gasp brought him back to reality.

Clygon had walked over to a large dark screen on the stage. He pulled the screen down, revealing Thomas Baxter, hung up like a starfish, his face bloodied and bruised.

"Dad!" Toby cried out.

Apparently, the Healer was free to move about and he immediately jumped up on the stage to attend to Thomas.

"Cut him down!" the Healer demanded.

Clygon simply smiled and nodded. Two troll soldiers cut the ropes and the Healer barely caught him, as Thomas fell to the floor semi-conscious. The Healer began to work his magic but Toby could see that his face was grim.

Suddenly, Toby felt himself engulfed by a hurricane. Intense red light radiated out of him.

"Dad!" he cried out again, with such despair and force that the walls of the hall shook.

His head filled with a rush of wind as he lunged toward Clygon. Clygon opened his arms to absorb Toby's anger. But Clovor held him back. He turned on her, his face full of rage, forcing Clovor to take a step back, which was all she could take since she was tied to him.

Toby was in full Hulk mode. Angry. Afraid. Helpless.

He didn't hear, or chose to ignore, the urgent voice in his head: *Be WISE Toby!*

Nor did he hear Buddy's apology before Buddy knocked him to the ground.

22

Silent Night

Toby knelt on all fours. For the second time that day, the breath had been knocked out of him. More than that, his will, his fight, his life, had been knocked out of him. He'd lost. Clygon had won. The first time around, he'd been lucky. Today proved he was no HERO. Period. Game over.

He hadn't noticed Clovor kneeling next to him, their hands still bound together. *Duh! If he hit the deck, then she hit the deck.*

The hall collectively held its breath, waiting to see what would happen next.

"Dad!" he sobbed. "Dad!"

"Toby, look at me," Clovor demanded. "This isn't over. Remember what the giant…"

"The giant is dead," he hissed at her. "Look at him. He can't help us any more."

But when he looked over to the giant's body, the giant was gone.

"He's not dead, Toby. You just heard him…"

"No, Clovor, he's… Wait… how did you…"

"I heard him, too, right before Buddy kindly bought us a few moments to figure out what to do next."

"He's dead, Clovor. And if he's not dead then he revived himself and abandoned…"

The compass in his pocket began to buzz. He ignored it.

"I'm giving in, Clovor. I know anger will only make Clygon stronger. So I'm giving up. I'm telling Clygon he wins. What else can I do? The Sword is in pieces. The giant is dead. And I'm no HERO. Maybe I can make a deal with him to let…"

The compass buzzed more aggressively.

"…to let you all go. To let Dad go…"

He angrily reached into his pocket and grabbed the compass.

"What!" he yelled at it.

As he watched the compass spinning wildly—W-I-S-E... W-I-S-E... W-I-S-E...—he heard the voice. The voice of his grandpa.

I've not abandoned you, Toby. I'm right here. My spirit is in you now. Remember when I blew my breath onto you? That was to ensure that I would always be with you. Now, dig deep into the hope within you and keep your eye on the compass. You have an important task before you. Think Scrooge, Toby.

Toby willed himself to calm down. No easy task with his dad in whatever shape he was in, off to the side of his vision.

The compass stopped spinning and landed on W—*Be Curious.*

Clovor saw it too.

"Remember," she whispered, "when the giant asked you why you think Clygon is the way he is? Remember how he suggested that curiosity might help you stand against him?"

"Okay, but how?"

At that moment, a small, orange Ostern egg rolled under Toby's legs. Then the red one. Then the blue one, subtly helped along by Buddy's foot.

Clovor handed him the orange egg, the one with the single triangle on it. It was soft and squishy. Toby absently squeezed it again and again as he thought.

"What do I do with it?"

The answer came instantly when Toby squeezed the egg a bit too hard, blowing the top—*or was it the bottom*—off of it. An orange vapor slowly seeped out of it, engulfing the two of them...

...they stood on a hill overlooking a battle below. Trolls vs river elves. River elves vs trolls.

"I know of this battle," Clovor said.

As she surveyed the scene, she gasped. "Grandpa?" Toby saw a younger version of the man he had met the last time in *RiverHome.*

Then, something caught Toby's eye, something glowing in the distance. He couldn't make it out at first but instinctively knew what it was. The Sword. But who was...

"Grandpa Baxter?" It seemed weird to call him Grandpa Baxter as Grandpa was twelve at that moment.

"Toby, this is the battle where..."

Their attention was drawn to a strong, muscle-bound Conan the Barbarian-looking troll, hammering his way through river elf soldiers, knocking them down one-by-one. Alongside him, fought an equally daunting troll woman.

Toby could see the resemblance of Clygon's nose to that of "Conan's" and Clygon's steely eyes in the woman.

"Are those Clygon's…"

…a fierce charge from the river elves…the two trolls disappeared under the surge… they didn't get back up again.

A cry of victory went up from the river elves.

"Claygon is dead! Slygon is dead!"

The troll retreat was in full swing…

…they were now near a pyre holding two bodies: Claygon and Slygon. Off to the side, alone, his head buried in his hands stood Clygon. He looked to be about five or six. A torch lit the pyre and Clygon cried out. As he did, a group of young trolls walked over and knocked him down, laughing as they walked away… was one of those trolls a young Plythar?

…now, they stood in the corner of what appeared to be a massive troll house… *is this where they make cookies?*… a party of some sort was going on. The house looked like it was decorated for Christmas. A huge feast filled a table around which sat at least a dozen trolls.

Toby was grateful that this was a vision because the troll stink must have been overwhelming, no matter how delicious the feast smelled.

"Where is my idiot brother's idiot son? We need more ale!" said a massive, blubbery troll at the head of the table, as he let out a big burp.

A ten or eleven-year-old Clygon walked in, carrying a tray of mugs, too many mugs for one person to handle. One of the guests stuck out his leg, tripping Clygon, who proceeded to dump all of the ale onto his uncle. While the others around the table roared in laughter, the uncle charged Clygon and slapped him so hard across the face that Clygon fell backwards onto the table, breaking it in half—food flying everywhere. He awkwardly struggled to his feet, rage on his face, and ran from the room. Toby couldn't help but remember when Derrick had tripped him in the lunchroom a few months ago…

…then they were outside. Snow covered everything. They could hear lots of shouting and cheering and laughter. A banner off to the side read: *251st Annual Rain-Dear Games!* Toby noticed deer roaming the area and wondered if the sign was misspelled. *I'm on break. No grammar. That includes spelling.*

Whatever these games were, they actually looked like fun. Toby was particularly intrigued by a game of American football being played by trolls on ice skates. Who'd have thought trolls could skate? He'd have to try that at his cousin's place in Wisconsin when they go to see them at New Year's. *If he gets out of this place alive.*

A young, buff teenage Clygon stood off to the side, alone.

"Don't tell me," Toby groaned. "They wouldn't let him join in any Rain-Dear Games."

Clovor poked him with her elbow. "Stay curious, Toby!"

Dejected, Clygon walked away from the games.

And Toby, against his will, began to feel sorry for him…

…now they were in the woods, the troll village still within sight. A lonely figure sat on a log, rocking back and forth. He'd gained weight. Some of it muscle, some of it blubber. He'd obviously been on the wrong end of a fight. Tears ran down his angry, bruised cheeks as he muttered, "You will take me seriously. You'll see. You will take me seriously…"

…Toby was back on all fours. The hall still silent. Almost as if everyone was frozen in time.

He looked up at Clygon. He saw the menace. The anger. The meanness. The power. But he begrudgingly saw something else.

"Do you see it, Toby?" Clovor asked. "Clygon is a wounded man, just like Scrooge was. That's the reason for his anger."

"But that doesn't justify what he's done… to my dad… what he did to Mathilda… to the river elves. I can't…"

Toby could feel the anger building up again, ready to explode out of him, mixed with despair. *What am I supposed to do with this monster?*

"Toby Baxter!"

It was Clygon. "My patience has come to an end. But my benevolence knows no bounds. So, let's make this a fair fight. Plythar! Young Toby Baxter here seems to like swords. Find him a sword worthy of this battle."

Plythar grabbed a sword out of the sheath of a troll soldier standing nearby and threw it at Toby, who was still on all fours.

"Get up!" Plythar walked over and roughly pulled Toby to his feet, cutting the leather that bound his hand to Clovor's.

Clovor tried to grab the sword. "I'll fight you, Clygon. He's just a boy. He doesn't know how to fight."

Plythar knocked her out of the way. She hit the floor hard. Clygon laughed. The crowd cheered. Donold tried to break free of his shackles, only

120

to receive a sword butt to the groin. Judah, Blythar, and Deckor all grimaced at the same time and moved into a groin-protecting stance.

"Pick up the sword and fight, HERO!"

Toby lifted the sword with both hands as Clygon charged him. How he ran with all of that blubber was a wonder, if Toby was in the mood for wonder. Which, apparently, he was supposed to be. With one mighty swing, Clygon swatted the sword out of Toby's hands, knocking him onto his back... on top of the broken Sword pieces.

The wolves howled. The unicorns whinnied and snorted, struggling to break free. Donold roared in anger and pain.

Clygon stood over Toby with his sword to Toby's neck.

The crowd chanted, Cly-gon! Cly-gon! Cly-gon!

He looked at his fans.

"What say ye? Thumbs up or thumbs down."

Toby looked up as best he could and saw a room full of thumbs down.

"I'm really going to enjoy this," Clygon whispered to Toby, drooling on him in the process.

But Toby felt the Sword fragments underneath him come alive, filling him with energy. He raised his hands, and instantly, a red, hot blaze burst out of him, throwing Clygon ten feet into the air. *That's 3.048 meters, give or take!*

He rolled onto his stomach in order to push himself to his feet when Clygon, recovering quickly, ran toward him and buried his massive foot into Toby's back.

And to think I was starting to feel some empathy for this guy!

Toby rolled over and threw his arms in front of his face, waiting for Clygon to bash his head in...

...when, suddenly, a huge wind swept through the hall. A sound like helicopters on steroids filled the place. Toby had heard that sound before.

Then he heard whooping and laughter coming from overhead.

"Toby! Toby! Up here! Catch!"

23

Joy to the World

Toby looked up and saw Sid... *Sid?... riding a dragon?, with Phoenix and Mathilda behind him riding on their own dragons?* Several drones flew alongside of them. In Sid's hands was *Loach* ablaze with light and energy.

Sid threw it down toward Toby. But the throw was just a bit off. He wasn't going to catch it. Then he remembered something from the footy game he participated in the last time he was in *RiverHome.* He jumped up and ran toward Clygon, whose back was to him, looking up at the dragons. He planted his knee into Clygon's back and launched himself into the air. One problem, among many at that moment: launching himself off of Clygon's back, was like launching off of a vat full of jello—green jello, with shredded carrots and fruit cocktail mixed in, known as salad in Minnesota. Immediately, he was off-kilter as he flew into the air.

Everything moved in slow motion. *Loach* turned over and over again. He needed to catch it by the handle, not the blade, obviously. He tried to adjust his trajectory as he reached out his arm. He had this. He was going to snatch *Loach* mid-air, land on his feet in a superhero crouch with his other hand planted on the ground, and then... and then...

...he missed the sword. Completely. And now he was spinning out of control. He landed with a thud on his back, *Loach* falling a foot away from him. The breath knocked out of him... again.

At first, no one moved.

Then Clygon yelled, "That's not possible. I destroyed the Sword! What is this trickery?"

He rushed forward to grab *Loach*...

...but somehow, Thomas Baxter got there first.

"Leave. My. Son. Alone!" he roared, pointing *Loach* at Clygon. Electric sparks moved up and down the sword.

Buddy ran over to Toby and helped him to his feet.

"Traitor!" yelled Oreeo from the side of the stage. But five ogre soldiers surrounded him and that shut him up.

"Dad! Are you okay?"

Thomas was bruised. He was winded. But his eyes were on fire.

"We've got this, son."

Thomas slowly edged over to Toby, his eyes on Clygon. He held out *Loach* so that, now, Toby and Thomas held the sword together. Toby could feel the sword's energy pulsating in his hand. He began to glow. So did his dad. Clygon backed away, calculating his next move.

"Stay where you are!" Toby demanded.

He looked at his dad. He saw the bruises. He saw him holding his ribs. He looked at Clygon. He felt his anger growing. His hands were glowing an angry red. He tried to aim *Loach* between Clygon's beady eyes, with the intent of... *of what? He needed to make Clygon pay, didn't he?* Everything in him wanted to hurt that troll.

"Do it, Toby! Do it!" Clygon goaded him, gaining energy from Toby's anger like the first time they had gone toe-to-toe.

"Not this way, Toby," his dad whispered.

The compass was now on overdrive in Toby's pocket. He took a deep breath. He pulled out the compass and glanced at it quickly simply to remind himself.

He'd done the Wonder bit. Check.

Service. He needed to start with kindness. No easy task.

Endurance. He needed to build on his last encounter with Clygon.

But how?

What am I missing?

Think, Toby. Think. Think Scrooge. Think... Scrooge. He ran the thought over and over in his mind.

Then an insight popped into his brain, metaphorically speaking.

"Clovor! The red Ostern egg. Squish it."

Clovor squeezed the egg and a red mist enveloped him, his dad, and Clygon.

"Okay... Think Scrooge," Toby said through the mist. "But... what does that mean?"

Come on, insight... come on!

"You haven't been reading *A Christmas Carol,* have you, son," Thomas whispered with a smile.

"Well… um… I read the first paragraph. But… um… it's a book… and I uh…"

"I get it, Toby. I wasn't a big book fan when I was your age either. Let's agree that you can read it when you get home. For now, here are the Cliff Notes: Scrooge was angry at the world. He'd been abandoned by his father. He was lonely. He lacked any kind of joy…"

At the word, joy, the red mist grew brighter and the vibe of *Loach* changed. Clygon noticed it first. His eyes widened with fear.

"No!" Clygon cried. "Not that! Stop them."

Then Toby noticed it. Then Thomas noticed it. Father and son looked at each other. Thomas grinned as he let go of *Loach*.

"Well," he whispered to Toby. "I didn't see that one coming."

"You've got to be kidding me!" was all Toby could say.

"You're on, Toby. I'm right next to you. So is Clovor. You got this," said Thomas.

Loach started to… *sing? A Christmas song? Are you having a laugh? It wants me to sing Christmas songs? That's the big insight?*

Toby looked around. *This is crazy.* But slowly, the singing of *Loach* filled him and he couldn't hold it in any longer…

"Dashing through the snow, in a one-horse open sleigh…" Everyone stared at him as if he had lost his mind. Except for Clygon. Clygon looked like he was in the midst of a meltdown.

"Or'e the fields we go, laughing all the way…"

A few people sang out: "Ha, ha, ha."

By now, Clygon was holding his hands over his ears shouting, "No Christmas music! Not that. I can't take it. Stop. No Christmas music! It's inhumane! It's worse than an Echo Egg!"

Clovor joined in. So did Thomas. So did Deckor. And Judah. And Oreea. And the ogres, gnomes, and trolls of the Resistance.

"Bells on bob tails ring, making spirits bright…"

What's a bob tail and why does it make spirits bright?

"Oh what fun it is to sing a sleighing song tonight…"

Toby kept his eyes glued on Clygon. The troll was in obvious distress.

"Ohhhhhh," the crowd held out the note, "Jingle bells, jingle bells, jingle all the way, oh what fun it is to ride in a one horse open sleigh…"

As the song ended Clygon removed his hands from his ears only to be assaulted by another carol, this time started by Oreea.

"Deck the halls with boughs of holly, Fa la la la la, la la la la…"

"No fa la la's! Stop. Stop them!" he cried to his soldiers. But when a few of them tried to move, the Resistance soldiers held them at bay.

"'Tis the season to be jolly, Fa la la la la, la la la la..."

The song finished and the singing stopped.

Clygon looked around. His breathing was heavy. But the brief reprieve seemed to revive him. He grabbed his sword which had fallen to the ground...

"Uh oh. We need to keep singing," Toby whispered to Clovor.

Clygon charged him.

But Toby was saved by... a drum solo. To the *Little Drummer Boy,* filled with pa rum pum pum pums. The wolves and unicorns kept time.

Clygon fell to his knees, crying out in agony, "No pa rum pum pums!" He clamped his hands over his ears but something was happening to him, and he couldn't stop it.

From above, the clear, bell-like sound of Sid's voice, rang through the air.

"Jolly old St. Nicholas, lean your ear this way..."

As he sang, friends and enemies joined in, swaying to the song, bright, cheerful smiles exchanged as they looked from one to another. It was like a scene from one of those *Hallmark* Christmas movies his Grandma Baxter loved to watch. All. Year. Long.

"Don't you tell a single soul, what I'm going to say..."

By now the band kicked in. Horribly. Playing the song in two or three different keys. Although the drummer was really good. But nobody seemed to mind.

In the midst of the singing, Toby yelled to Clovor: "The blue egg. I need to see Clygon's future."

As the blue mist surrounded him, he saw it.

"Seriously?"

The song came to an end and no one chimed in with a new one.

Silence. And then...

Clygon shrieking.

"I'm shrinking! I'm shrinking!"

And before their eyes, Clygon began to shrink.

24

A Baby Changes Everything

It was like a scene out of the *Wizard of Oz*. That moment when Dorothy threw water on the Wicked Witch of the East—*or was it West?... no... it was East*—and the water melted her.

Were they actually destroying Clygon? *Am I destroying Clygon?*

The hall went still.

Everyone held their breath. And watched.

But Clygon wasn't actually shrinking. He was regressing. He was growing younger. *Is growing younger an oxymoron? And what is an oxymoron?*

That's the future Toby had seen.

Now, Clygon was the buff teenager Toby and Clovor had watched in the vision of Clygon's past... Now, he was a young boy... Now, he was a baby, his small baby troll head sticking out of the big fur robe he had been wearing a moment before as an adult.

Toby feared Clygon would regress into nothingness but the transformation stopped. Clygon was now a crying twelve-pound baby.

Nobody moved.

Toby looked at Clovor. And then at Buddy. And then at Plythar. And then at the crowd.

"I didn't mean to... this wasn't... I... I'm sorry... I..."

A loud cheer broke out. From almost everyone.

Toe-bee! Toe-bee! Toe-bee!

Clovor ran over and put her arm around him, encouraging the crowd with her other arm to keep up the cheering.

"You freed them from Clygon's tyranny. That's why they're cheering, Toby. You did it."

"But Clygon... he's... what did I do?"

126

Oreea made her way over to baby Clygon. During the carol singing, Buddy had slipped over and released her and the other captives.

She picked up the baby and held him to her shoulder, gently rubbing his back, trying to calm the crying. Clygon spit up on her tunic. Greenish, mucusy spit up. *Gross!*

"Toby," she said, dabbing the spit-up off with a napkin handed to her by Clovor, who was busy making faces at the baby. "You have given Clygon a second chance. A chance to know love. To know joy. To be a different person. I'll make sure I find a good family for him." She hugged baby Clygon to her. "You've given him a new beginning. And with that, a new beginning for the trolls."

"By singing Christmas songs? That's…"

"That's what?" Clovor asked.

But now, Oreea was barking out orders.

"Buddy," she commanded, "have the Resistance come to me."

Out of the crowd, poured what looked like a hundred troll and ogre soldiers.

"Arrest my brother and his followers!"

Immediately, four Resistance soldiers nabbed Oreeo and those loyal to him.

"Daiseea," she called out to a female ogre soldier. "Go and release the Prime Minister. As his new Captain of the Guard, I am restoring the good name of *Ogreton Heights*. Once again, we stand on the side of peace, thanks to the wise and heroic actions of Toby Baxter. Hip hip hooray! Hip hip hooray!"

But Toby was walking his dad back to the Healer. With the exception of a black eye and a few bruises, Thomas seemed in good spirits.

"I'm proud of you, son!"

"Dad, when did you get here? Why is Sid here?"

Apparently, the dragons had landed because Sid came running up and hug-tackled Toby.

The band started playing again. Still badly, except for the drummer. "I saw three ships come sailing in on Christmas day on Christmas day…"

The river elf cousins and their friends hugged and high-fived each other.

Sid showed Toby the green mark on his hand and tried to explain why he was wearing a Packer's helmet.

Mathilda and Phoenix ran over and patted Sid on the back, talking over each other about what it was like to fly on a dragon.

127

Donold put his hand on Toby's shoulder. "A line in the sand. And now Christmas carols! What's next, a break-dancing competition?" He shook his head, laughed, and headed over to check on the unicorns.

Saaba jumped up on Toby and licked his face from chin to forehead and Saanti did the same to Thomas.

Judah, not so subtly, made his way to Oreea to ask if he could help. She handed him baby Clygon and ran off to welcome back the Prime Minister.

"What am I supposed to do with…" But then baby Clygon nestled his head in Judah's shoulders. And for some strange reason, Judah wept.

The snow fell.

Carols were sung.

The lights glowed.

Friends and enemies called a truce.

A spirit-like, snowy-white giant caught Toby's attention and gave him a thumbs up, and then disappeared.

And for a few moments, there was peace on earth.

***

Toby made his way over to Judah, noticing Judah wiping his cheek.

"You okay?"

"Just something irritating my eye."

"Uh huh…" Toby smiled.

He circled around to look into the face of baby Clygon. The baby looked at him, smiled, and bopped him on the nose. And almost knocked Toby off of his feet.

***

"Disgusting!" muttered Plythar. "Sickening."

Plythar angrily played with the sword in his hand, pacing back and forth just out of sight of the "makes-me-want-to-gag" love fest inside.

"Plythar!" Blythar said, a bit out of breath after tracking down his brother. "Why are you so angry? Isn't this what we were working for?"

Plythar glared at him. "We lost. Again!" The words came out like vomit.

"But… but… I thought you were on our side? You gave me this Esther egg!"

"I stole it out of the dead fingers of a traitor troll!"

"What? Why?"

"Why? Because I wanted to see those smug Baxters and their little friends put in their place once and for all. So, I manipulated the situation in Clygon's favor. But Clygon proved to be weak. Again. Just like he did when he was a kid. He's brought shame onto the trolls. Again. And I intend to erase that shame."

Blythar took a step back from his brother's rage. But Plythar grabbed him by the tunic.

"Join me, Blythar."

"What?" Blythar tried to pull away, but Plythar held him.

"Be my right-hand troll, brother. We can control the trolls now. We can rebuild the army. Because this is not over! The trolls will rise up to fight another day."

"No, Plythar! We have a chance to stop the hatred. To stop the bloodshed. To let our folk live in peace."

Plythar pushed him away. "You're just as weak as Clygon. Go sing your insipid..."

"Insipid? That's a big word for you, brother," Blythar said, trying to inject some humor.

Plythar grunted, turned, and marched out into the darkness, a group of thirty trolls following behind him.

25

Let There Be Peace on Earth

"To Toby Baxter!" Oreea shouted.

"To Toby Baxter!" the crowd responded as they lifted their goblets in a toast. *Why is it called a toast when it has nothing to do with bread?*

Things had moved quickly. Oreea and the Prime Minister, representing the ogres, met with Donold and Clovor, representing the river elves, Blythar, representing the trolls, and Jerry and Roxie, representing the gnomes and wolves, to hammer out a peace and trade agreement. No one expected it to be easy. They knew Plythar was angry and on the loose. But they didn't want to waste the moment.

As a part of the agreement, the ogres announced that their traveling circus would return to *RiverHome* in a few months. The three unicorns, Hermey, Philly, and Raypha, agreed to be a part of the show as the ogres promised to treat them humanely.

Prothar, Sythar, and Thytar approached Toby, with Sythar carrying baby Clygon, who was starting to look weirdly like baby Yoda. Toby took a few steps back, wary of baby Clygon's left hook.

"Oreea has given us charge of Clygon," Prothar said, beaming like a proud troll dad. "We promise you, Toby, he will be raised in love to be a good troll. We will do you proud, and one day, Clygon will do you proud, too."

Toby wasn't so sure.

He, his dad, and Sid spent much of the time answering Sid's questions. Unlike Toby and Thomas, who had been eased into the story, Sid had been thrown in head-first. He still had a sense that it was all a dream.

Now, the hall, which had witnessed the dramatic showdown between Clygon and Toby, served as a banquet hall. The food looked like a picture out of a holiday magazine: turkey, mashed potatoes, cranberries, green bean and mushroom soup casserole, green jello with shredded carrots and fruit cocktail mixed in, dinner rolls, and lots of sparkling apple ale.

The hall itself glowed with candle lights and torches under a clear sky, with a full moon. It was cold, but everyone had been supplied with warm ogre coats.

After an official greeting from the Prime Minister and a prayer of thanksgiving led by Clovor, Oreea called out the toast to Toby.

As the guests raised their glasses and cheered him, Toby's face turned bright red.

"I really didn't do…"

"Don't!" Mathilda put her pointer finger in front of his face. "Don't go there. You did that last time. Look around you, Toby. And enjoy it. This is your moment. But it's also a new moment for all of us. So, let us say our thanks so we can eat."

Toby's dad nudged him and smiled. "You never get used to it."

The food tasted as good as it looked. And Drummer's band sounded as terrible as it did earlier, as they tried to play Christmas music, although Drummer was outstanding.

After the festivities, they all headed to bed. Toby hadn't realized how exhausted he was. Just as he was about to fall asleep, Saaba walked in and curled up next to him. Sid's gentle snoring in the bed across the room provided some white noise, and soon, Toby was fast asleep. *Loach*, on a table near the room's window, glowed quietly.

***

Toby slowly opened his eyes. Saaba was still asleep. Sid was gone. The light in the room was bright. He yawned. He stretched. He rolled out of bed.

Just as he did, his dad walked in. The bruise on his face had turned purple and yellow.

"Mom's going to ask a lot of questions," Toby laughed.

"And she's going to get quite a story," Dad replied. "Get dressed, son. I let you sleep in. Everyone is packed and ready to head back to *RiverHome*."

Saaba's ears perked up. He yawned. He stretched. He rolled out of bed and headed out of the room, presumably to find Jerry.

Once dressed, Toby grabbed *Loach* and followed his dad out into the big hall.

Blythar, Prothar, Sythar, and Thytar, who was holding baby Clygon, along with a large group of trolls, huddled around Toby and Thomas and said their goodbyes. Clygon took another swing at Toby, thankfully, missing him this time. Everyone laughed except Toby and Thomas. Something didn't seem right…

Jerry, a group of gnomes, Saaba, Saanti, and a group—*or is it pack*—of wolves, were the next to surround Toby and Thomas.

"On behalf of Chieftain Ernest and the gnomes, friend Toby, thank you once again for being our HERO."

"But I didn't really…" Thomas nudged him before he could finish.

"And Friend Thomas, it was good to see you again." Jerry and the gnomes bowed to them. Saaba, Saanti, and the wolves did likewise. Then, Saaba jumped up on Toby and gave him a big, sloppy lick. Toby hugged the wolf with tears in his eyes.

Sid came running over yelling, "Come on, Toby! You won't want to miss this. Come on!" He grabbed Toby by the arm and tried to drag him through the hall, Thomas walking behind.

But they were stopped by Oreea.

Immediately, Toby sensed something was wrong with Sid. He'd completely stopped breathing. His eyes were glued on Oreea.

"He's got a bit of a crush on her," Thomas whispered to him.

"Thomas, Toby, and Sid…"

Sid sighed when she said his name.

"On behalf of the ogres, thank you. We will always hold you in high esteem. Travel safe, my friends."

Toby and Thomas moved to go but had to turn back to grab Sid, who was rooted in his spot, his gaga face rooted on Oreea.

"Sid! Snap out of it. You told me there's something I don't want to…"

The sound of helicopters on steroids filled the hall, as did the wind from the flapping of three flying dragons. They landed outside the hall where Toby, Thomas, and Sid found them, along with the river elves. Not far from them, was the sleigh that had brought Clovor and Toby to *Ogreton Heights*. Next to the sleigh, were the three unicorns.

"Ready to head back to *RiverHome*?" Deckor asked.

"*Loach* is telling me it's time," Toby said. "Speaking of the Sword, what about…"

"Got it!" Mathilda said. She hoisted up the bag holding the broken pieces of the Sword.

"What will you do with it?" Thomas asked.

"Not sure yet," Phoenix said. "We'll figure that out another day."

"Let's go!" Donold said impatiently.

"How are we getting there?" Toby asked.

"The unicorns have agreed to drive the sleigh down the mountain," Donold answered. "Clovor, the Healer, and I will ride with them and then travel by foot the rest of the way."

"And you, Toby," Sid could hardly contain himself, "will be flying back first class on Billie, here."

Toby's eyes grew wide.

"I... get to... ride... on a dragon? Are you kidding me?"

"Mathilda will ride with you. Thomas, you will ride on Ruphas..." Ruphas nodded to Thomas..."along with Deckor, and I'll be riding on Dahrlah with Phoenix."

"What about Judah?" Thomas asked.

"I'm... uh... er... um... staying here for a while to see if I can... um... uh... be of assistance to the... uh... ogres..."

"You mean a certain ogre, don't you?" teased Phoenix.

Toby saw Sid make a not-so-nice face at Judah.

"Then, I guess this is goodbye," Toby said as he hugged Judah. "We will miss you!"

Judah shook hands with Thomas and a begrudging Sid, hugged his sister and cousins, and headed back to the hall.

"See you later, lover boy," Phoenix called after him.

"Toby," Clovor grabbed him by the arm. "Just in case Donold and I don't get back in time... it's been quite an adventure!" She gave Toby a big hug and then did the same to Thomas and Sid.

Donold stood in front of Toby and smiled.

"You are a good soldier, Toby. You stayed true to yourself." He stuck out his hand, shook Toby's, and drew him in for a hug.

As the others said their goodbyes, Toby turned to Billie. She remembered him. She reached out her massive wing and cradled him in a hug. Once again, Toby lost his composure. Before he knew it, he was sitting comfortably behind her head, Mathilda behind him. He lay *Loach* carefully across his lap.

"Put this on," Mathilda said.

It was an LA Rams helmet.

"No way am I wearing that..."

Mathilda stuffed it on his head.

"Where do I hold…" But suddenly, they were in the air. He let out an involuntary woo-hoo and started giggling. Mathilda laughed behind him.

As he looked down, he yelled, "This is… this is…" But he couldn't find the words. *Apparently, Author was sleeping again. Or maybe there are experiences where the emotion is enough.*

They flew down the mountain into the plains. The weather changed quickly from snow to spring. The lifelessness Toby had seen just days ago had been transformed, no doubt the work of *Loach.*

Occasionally, Billie would tuck in her wings and soar straight up, leaving Toby's stomach in his feet, and then, dive down, pulling up just before hitting the trees. Normally, this would have been frightening, but Mathilda's constant humming and the security Billie provided, made it a flight he'd always remember.

It was over all too quickly.

They gently landed on the playing pitch to a crowd of river elves. As they cheered and applauded, Toby couldn't help himself. He held *Loach* high above his head, causing the crowd to cheer all the more. He felt like a gold medalist. And then he felt embarrassed.

He found himself back down on terra firma. *Terra firma? Now you show up with big words?* Billie, once again, wrapped her wing around him and gave him a big hug. He returned the hug, and then, slowly backed away. Billie winked at him, spread out her massive wings, and along with Ruphas and Dahrlah, bolted back into the sky.

He felt two very small, thin arms around his waist.

"Toby," Grandma said. "I knew you would do it."

She reached out her arm and grabbed Thomas. "I could not be more proud of the two of you. And you, Sid, come here, my son." A group hug.

"Where's Judah?"

It was Roxie, having hugged and kissed Phoenix.

"He stayed in *Ogreton Heights.* He's in love!"

"With Oreea, I'll bet. How sweet."

Sid growled.

Toby heard a loud squaaaaawk! and looked up to see Hiriam, Demetrius, and five other drones circling overhead.

Loach started to buzz in Toby's hand.

Grandma sensed it and said, "I have dinner prepared. We best be going."

During dinner, they told stories of the last few days, they laughed, and talked about what this new era of peace might bring.

Phoenix suddenly jumped up and said, "I have an announcement to make." He checked his pockets but whatever he was looking for wasn't there. "Just a minute…"

He ran down the hallway to his bedroom and was back in two shakes. *Two shakes? Really?*

He was holding what looked like a multi-colored plastic egg. When Mathilda saw it, she gasped.

"It's an Agape Egg," Mathilda whispered to Toby. "A love egg."

Phoenix cleared his throat and got down on one knee. "Um, Roxie, I was… um… wondering… if you might… would you… ah… would you marry me?"

He opened the egg, revealing a simple, plain-looking ring. But from the look on Roxie's face, it could have been made of gold.

She ran over and jumped onto Phoenix, knocking him onto his back.

"Yes, Phoenix, I will marry you!"

Saanti joined in the fun by diving onto Phoenix and Roxie and everyone around the table applauded.

"To Phoenix and Roxie," Deckor said.

"To Phoenix and Roxie," the rest said as they drank a toast to them, once again, without bread.

Mathilda noticed the look on Toby's face.

"What is it?"

He nodded toward *Loach*.

"I think our time here is done."

The room fell silent. There wasn't much more to be said.

"We'll walk with you," Mathilda said.

"Before you go," Grandma said, "get in a circle."

They joined hands as Grandma stood in the middle. The river elves began their Celtic humming. Toby could feel the energy, as he always did during these moments.

Grandma raised her hands.

"Go in peace. Go in joy. And may you sense the grace of your Creator and the love of your *RiverHome* friends."

The humming faded slowly and they released hands.

Grandma hugged Thomas, then Sid, then Toby as they walked out the door into the night.

Toby, Thomas, Sid, Deckor, Mathilda, Phoenix, Roxie, and Saanti, made their way to the Sword's monument. *Loach* was buzzing, as if in anticipation of going home.

Toby walked up the monument and held the sword in the air. *Loach's* glow enveloped him and the rest of the group, bringing a sense of deep calm and peace. He turned the sword with its point facing downward and put it back into the monument. Light began to radiate into the monument and out into the ground. They could feel its life-nourishing power under their feet.

Toby jumped off the stone and joined the rest of them, as they made their way down the hill toward the waterfall and the portal on the other side of the stream.

The portal was open.

Mathilda threw her arms around Toby. "I hate this. I hate saying goodbye!"

She let go and moved on to Thomas, and then, to Sid.

They all said their goodbyes, and then, Toby, Thomas, and Sid crossed over the tree bridge and headed to the portal.

THIS ISN'T OVER, BAXTERS!

Plythar's voice was the last they heard before the portal closed.

26

Christmas Time is Here!

Toby heard voices. He was back in his own bed. The clock read eight a.m. He threw open the curtains and watched the large snowflakes as they descended on his backyard. He looked over the other side of his bed. Sid was still sound asleep. The place where *Loach* had hung on the wall, now empty.

He walked out into the kitchen.

"Mom! What are you doing here? I thought you wouldn't be home until tomorrow?"

She gave him what amounted to be her version of a stink eye.

"I can see from your father's face, and his explanation of what happened to his face, that you've made another trip to RiverTown. And you took Sid with you? What were you thinking? What if something had happened?"

Toby ran over and hugged her.

"It's good to see you too, Mom!"

"All right…. All right… give me some space and I'll get the Christmas pancakes going."

"Wait! Is it Christmas today?" Toby asked.

"No," his dad said, "it's the morning after you headed to *RiverHome.* But mom figures you and Sid could use some early Christmas pancakes."

"We sure could," said Sid, scratching his right hand. "You would not believe the dream I had last night. It was the most weirdest…"

"You don't put a most before a word ending in -est," Toby interrupted. *Now I'm correcting grammar?*

"Huh?" said Sid.

He looked down and saw the green line on his hand. He looked at Toby. He looked at Mr B. He looked at Mrs B.

A big smile broke out on his face.

"It wasn't a dream, was it! I really flew a dragon! Woo-hoo! Just wait until my mom…"

"Slow down, Sid," Thomas said. "Mrs B, here, is still trying to get her brain around this. And she's had a few months. So perhaps we need to take things slowly. Let's ease your mom into it."

They spent the rest of the day decorating the house. A tree in the living room. One in the basement TV room. A small one in Toby's bedroom. Dad put up the lights outside, and over a cup of hot chocolate, they put the star on top of the living room tree. Then, they hit the switch and it was officially Christmas time in the Baxter household.

They finished out the evening by watching the 1971 movie, *Scrooge!* on Amazon. The giant was right. It was a good movie. Although Toby wasn't quite sure the Ghost of Christmas Present was as spot on as the Christmas Giant said. But all in all, great music. A good story. And best of all, now Toby didn't have to read the book.

***

Church could sometimes be boring. But for the most part, Toby loved his church. The youth director made things fun and interesting. And the Sunday services weren't bad. The music was upbeat. And the pastor preached short sermons! Tolerable.

But Christmas Eve was always a don't miss! The church looked like a Christmas wonderland inside and out. The music department pulled out all of the stops with *O, Holy Night… Joy to the World… I Heard the Bells on Christmas Day… and Silent Night,* during which everyone held lighted candles. The crunching of the snow under their feet after the service, in the quiet darkness, brought a magical end to the service.

In the days prior to Christmas Eve, Toby and Sid spent most of their time sliding off of the roof of Toby's house and reading *Marvel* comic books. Sometimes, warming up over a cup of hot chocolate, they would tell Toby's mom about their adventures in *RiverHome.* She would try to smile but the panic behind her eyes said something else.

Before the nine p.m. Christmas Eve Service, Toby's family enjoyed a Christmas meal at Sid's house. Sid's mom had insisted on it after the kindness the Baxters had shown them over the last several months. Toby and his parents left around eight, so that Sid, his mom, and his sister, could FaceTime Sid's dad before church.

The Christmas tradition in the Baxter household was to open a few gifts after the Christmas Eve service and the rest on Christmas Day after Santa had made his yearly visit. Grandma Baxter would join them for Christmas Day brunch, they would open gifts, and then, in the afternoon, Sid was coming back over. The Arizona Cardinals had the Christmas afternoon game.

Toby and his mom and dad sat by the tree after the Christmas Eve service. It was just as peaceful and quiet as you would expect on such a night. It even started to snow again, right on time. *How in the world did people celebrate Christmas without snow!*

Finally, Dad stood up and headed to the tree.

"Hmmm…"

"Hmmm, what?" Mom asked.

"Come here and take a look."

Toby and his mom joined Thomas at the tree. It took a moment, but then they saw it… or rather them. Buried in the Christmas tree were… *Easter eggs?*

"How did those get there?" Mom asked.

Toby looked around for signs of Author. Nothing.

"Toby, did you do this?"

Toby smiled innocently. Mom hugged him.

"You always like to surprise, don't you!"

They opened their gifts, drank some hot chocolate, read the Christmas Story from Luke chapter two, said a prayer together, and then headed to bed.

"Toby, I'm going to finish up *A Christmas Carol tonight.* Do you want to join me?"

"I thought watching the movie…"

"There's no substitute for a book, Toby," Mom said as she headed into her room.

Toby had a lot of skimming to do.

Having seen the movie helped, because the old English of the book was a challenge.

He read about the Miser Scrooge, the ghost of Christmas past, the ghost of Christmas present (apparently the Christmas Giant), the ghost of Christmas yet-to-come, and the transformation of Scrooge from an old crank to a man full of joy.

He thought about Clygon and hoped his new family would raise him with joy.

He thought about Derrick.

I wonder if there's hope for him?

There's always hope, Toby.

The voice of his grandpa.

He saw something glowing out of his window. The Christmas Giant's big radiant spirit-face filled the window. He smiled and disappeared.

Toby skipped to the end of the book. He could barely keep his eyes open.

...and it was always said of him, that he knew how to keep Christmas well, if any man alive possessed the knowledge. May that be truly said of us, and all of us! And so, as Tiny Tim observed, God Bless Us, Every One!

Toby Baxter had fallen asleep.

Epilogue—(Really)

My Favorite Things

Humming woke him. He recognized the tune. A song from *The Sound of Music.*

Sure enough, Author sat at the end of his bed, glowing. He'd changed out his Christmas Sweater for another one, which was even more hideous, if that were possible... *or is it, if that was possible? Come on, Author, it's Christmas!...* a Santa hat covering his bald head, and his standard notebook, pencil, and reading glasses.

"Merry Christmas, Toby!"

"Merry Christmas, Author!" Toby replied as he sat up.

Author continued to hum the song.

"Um," interrupted Toby, "that's not really a Christmas song."

"It's not?"

"No, it's from a movie called, *The Sound of Music.*"

"And?"

"Well. They sing it when they're afraid of a storm, not at Christmas. So, you might want to scratch that one from your top twenty favorite Christmas songs..." But Toby was laughing as he said it. Kind of.

"Quite a Christmas Adventure you had," Author said, changing the subject. "And bringing young Sid along—a stroke of genius."

"That was my dad's doing."

"Regardless, it added a nice layer to the story."

"So... is this the Epilogue?"

"Good catch, Toby. It's actually our second go of it, if you remember."

"It is?"

"By the way, did you get the Easter Eggs in the Christmas tree? I told you they are all the rage in stories, songs, and movies..."

"Yah, but I still don't think that's what they mean by Easter Eg..."

"So, it looks to me like you've wrapped up your *RiverHome* story."

Toby's face fell. *Can a face fall?*

"Really? That's it?" Toby didn't try to hide the disappointment. "Kind of ruins Christmas, doesn't it?"

Author stared a Toby for a moment. Then he smiled and jotted a few notes in his notebook.

"Clygon may be getting a new start…"

"May be?…"

"A tentative peace treaty has been signed by the trolls, ogres, gnomes, and river elves…"

"Tentative?…"

"Phoenix and Roxie are hopefully getting married…"

"Hopefully?…"

Author wrote down a few more notes. Then he looked up at Toby, sat back, and smiled.

"Well, maybe it doesn't sound completely wrapped up after all."

He winked at Toby.

"Is this a new cliffhanger?"

Author started humming again.

"Wait a minute!" Toby bolted upright.

"The penny has dropped," Author said as he wrote in his notebook.

"The what did what?" Toby asked.

"You've not heard that phrase before? It comes from Britain in the 1930s. Sometimes a penny would get stuck in the pressing machine, causing it to jam up. The operator would have to wait for the stuck penny to drop onto the floor before the machine would work…"

"Is this an excurses? And where have I heard that word before?"

"So, when the penny drops, that means you finally see something or understand it. So, as you were saying, Toby?"

Toby forgot what he was saying. He needed the penny to drop again.

And then it did. Kind of.

"Plythar! He said something just as we were headed back. He said… he said…"

Author finished for him, saying the words and writing them at the same time:

"This isn't over, Baxters!"

Toby shivered.

"What does that mean?"

"Merry Christmas, Toby. That's my Christmas gift to you. A new quest... Oh, and this."

Author handed Toby a giant Easter Egg.

"Author, thanks, but as I said, this isn't what it means to... Wait! Is this solid chocolate?"

Toby pulled back some of the foil and took a big bite off of the top of the egg. He re-wrapped it and put the egg on the floor, eased back down into his pillow, and closed his eyes as the chocolate melted in his mouth.

Tomorrow is Christmas Day!

Author hummed *My Favorite Things*.

"Not a Christmas song," Toby mumbled as he fell asleep.

In the closet, a bag began to glow.

The End.

Toby Baxter will be back in a new adventure:

The *GOOD* Prophecy

It was still dark but Toby thought he could see the faint outline of light breaking in. The tour guide explained that the ride was 24 miles downhill. They would stop at various points along the road to enjoy the views and learn some history. Toby was glad he had some warm clothes because it was cold! The guide assured them they'd heat up soon enough.

They'd be riding mountain bikes equipped with special brakes that could handle the steep 6500-foot drop from start to finish. It had a much different feel from his bike at home but Toby could tell this was going to be epic.

Toby's mom walked over and hugged him, and then Sid. "I'm kind of nervous," she whispered to the two of them. "It's been a long time since I've ridden a bike. The last time was years ago. Mr B and I were on a group bike ride in Washington D.C. at the end of a week-long bike trip that started in Gettysburg. Unfortunately, I misjudged the space between two metal pylons right in front of the Lincoln Memorial. I crashed and badly bruised my ribs. It was a long flight home that afternoon! So, you boys keep me safe, okay?"

They climbed onto their bikes. The sun was just starting to peek out on the horizon.

"Let's go!" the tour guide yelled. Slowly, one by one, they lifted their feet off of the ground, placed them on the pedals, and started to coast down the volcano into the sunrise.

Toby couldn't believe how peaceful it was. And how breathtaking. As he looked to his right he noticed that they were actually above the clouds, the sun turning them a bright orange.

This would be a good time to practice some vocabulary words... He could hear Mrs Grayson's voice in his head... *Exhilarating... Invigorating... Stimulating... Wow! He really did need a vacation from school.*

Sid, being Sid, was woohooing and laughing and woohooing some more. Toby quickly looked back to see that Mom had a big smile on her face, but he could tell that her hands where millimetres away from the brakes. Dad rode up to Toby and gave him a thumbs up before slowing down to get back in line behind Mom.

The sun was slowly rising as they quickly flew down the hill. Up ahead Toby could see a low-hanging cloud covering the road in front of them. *This was going to be cool! Riding into a cloud!*

Sid was the first into it, still woohooing, followed by Toby.

Toby instantly felt the cool mist from the cloud on his face. It stung a bit because of the cold. He found it a bit hard to see through the fog, so he slowed down, hoping Mom and Dad did he same. He could no longer hear Sid woohooing and wondered if the cloud muted sounds...*It did seem awfully quiet... And it seemed to be taking a long time to get to the other side of the cloud...* He felt a tinge of fear. Something didn't feel right. It grew much darker than he expected. In fact, too dark. It created the sense that he wasn't moving.

Then he realized that he wasn't moving. He was no longer on his bike. He was standing in complete darkness. A darkness so dark he that couldn't see his hand in front of his face. And the silence was deafening. *Can silence be deafening?* All he could hear was his breathing.

He stood still. He tried to calm himself. He reached out his hands. Nothing in front of him. He reached out to his sides. Still nothing. He reached up and stood on his toes. Still nothing.

He slowly moved to his left, his armed raised. It took several steps but he finally felt something solid. He took off his glove and felt a rough rock wall. He moved several steps to his right and felt the same thing.

He was in a cave.

What was he doing in a cave?

He began to panic. He could feel the walls closing in on him making him feel claustrophobic. He was about to scream...

...when he saw two green eyes coming toward him.

He held his breath. He closed his eyes... *like that was going to make him invisible.* He could hear whatever it was getting closer and closer...

... and then he felt a big slurpy lick across his face.

He recognized that lick. It was Saaba, Jerry the Gnome's faithful wolf!

What was he doing here?

Toby leaned down, reaching out his arms. Saaba snuggled up to him and Toby buried his head into the wolf and released his panic through his tears. But the tears didn't last long. He heard another noise. He looked up. He saw a light coming toward him. He heard a voice call out: "Saaba?"

Shivers raced up and down Toby's back. He knew that voice. It sounded younger. But there was no mistaking it.

Clygon!

Keep up on all things Toby Baxter by joining the mailing list at
www.TimWrightBooks.com.

Made in the USA
Monee, IL
02 November 2023

45353611R00083